IN THE COLD OF THE NIGHT

Published in 2016 by
Gritstone Publishing Co-operative
Birchcliffe Centre
Hebden Bridge
HX7 8DG
http://gritstone.coop

Gritstone Publishing Co-operative is jointly owned by its members, some
of Britain's best-regarded authors writing about the countryside and the
outdoors. Look out for our other titles.

© Andrew Bibby 2016
Typeset by Carnegie Book Production, Lancaster
Printed by Jellyfish Solutions Ltd
Cover photo © Steve Pipe, cumbrianrambler.blogspot.co.uk

ISBN 978-0-9955609-1-8

Catalogue in publication data is available from the British Library.

This is a work of fiction, and all the characters in this book are fictitious.
Any resemblance to actual persons, living or dead, is entirely coincidental.
Nevertheless there are, in the real world of the Lake District, teams of
volunteer mountain rescue teams ready to help those in the mountains
who get into difficulties. The author is choosing to make a contribution of
45p, representing 5% of this book's cover price, for each book sold to the
Langdale and Ambleside Mountain Rescue Team.

IN THE COLD OF THE NIGHT

by Andrew Bibby

GRITSTONE
PUBLISHING

Sunday

1.

There were occasions, Monica Roughlee reflected, when she could cheerfully have murdered her boss. This was one of those times.

She watched Richard Meade sitting a couple of rows ahead of her at the front of the minibus, talking interminably into his mobile. He must have started the conversation somewhere on the M74 travelling south towards the English border and here they were now, in a lane in the Lake District and he was still talking. God knew who he needed to talk to at this time of night.

Outside all was darkness and, presumably, mountains. It was late on Saturday evening – no, Monica corrected herself, it was already Sunday morning – and this was turning into the worst weekend of her life. The young lad Peter from the sales team, next to her in the minibus, had fallen asleep with his head perched intimately on her right breast. In the row ahead someone, maybe the secretary Raisha, was quietly snoring. Monica wriggled her toes in her walking boots. The boots had seemed fine in the shop when she'd bought them but she'd turned out to have acquired footwear with a deeply sadistic streak, boots which had delighted in giving her a set of matching blisters on each foot when she was only half way up Ben Nevis. Sometime soon, she thought, this minibus would park up and she'd have to clamber out and take her boots and her blisters, in the dark, up another bleeding mountain. And then tomorrow, always assuming she survived that long, there'd be a third mountain. Snowdon. Joy.

This was, of course, all the fault of Meade. He'd breezed into the office one day earlier in the year and announced that he'd had a good idea. A works outing with a difference, he said. "All in a good cause," he added. They were to tackle the Three Peaks challenge, he'd said, doing the three highest mountains in England, Scotland and Wales all in one weekend. In June, when the weather was always perfect. And they'd do it as a fundraiser for the local children's hospice, which was appealing for money to build a new extension.

The trip was, of course, entirely voluntary. Except of course, as always with her boss, it wasn't voluntary at all. Monica knew only one thing about the mountains of Britain and that was that she liked looking at them on Countryfile with a beer and her boyfriend Matt beside her at home but had no wish for any closer relationship with them. She pondered as the minibus lurched around a corner where Matt would be at that moment. He'd smirked a little when she'd told him of her weekend away and had muttered that he thought he might be able to persuade a few of his old mates to find something to do on a Saturday night. He'd better not be enjoying himself too much, she thought, elbowing the sleeping Peter beside her as some kind of revenge.

Of course she'd agreed to Meade's mad idea. And, of course, so had almost everyone else who worked at Greensleeves Park, the mobile homes place where she worked typing out the invoices for the pitch charges and hassling the poor old folks who'd thought they'd found their perfect retirement homes and hadn't realised how much Greensleeves would charge them for their little six-metres-by-five plot of heaven on earth. Of the staff only Jack Higgins the maintenance man, a couple of years short of retirement, had managed to avoid the weekend. "No, you're all right Mr Meade," he'd said with a sort-of smile.

So their names went up on the staff noticeboard for what was, apparently, to be a trip of a lifetime. Meade had had another brilliant idea. He'd offer a bottle of champagne, or maybe it would be Spanish cava, to the employee who got the most sponsorship, he said. This meant that for the past three months everyone had had to colour in on a roughly drawn outline of a mountain on a large sheet of paper exactly how much money they'd had pledged – and for the past three months everyone had been able to see that Monica had been the least successful. Of course, she wanted to raise money for the hospice, it was a cause dear to her heart. But apart from Matt who'd somewhat reluctantly offered her a tenner, she really didn't have very many friends with money to spare. And meanwhile Mr Meade himself, even though he'd excused himself from the colouring-in exercise, was dropping heavy hints on how much he'd raised. Three thousand pounds in a single evening in the golf club bar, apparently.

Looking at him again at the front of the minibus she suddenly felt an intense loathing towards the man she was dependent on if she wanted to keep her job. He was, of course, wearing all the right stuff for a weekend in the mountains. Monica knew almost nothing about the sort of clothing you needed for the great outdoors (although she'd been shocked at how much the cheapest waterproofs and boots had set her back when she'd bought them), but even Monica recognised that Meade hadn't stinted himself when it came to getting the fancy gear. He was clad head-to-foot in the very best performance clothing. In contrast her own flimsy waterproof still hadn't dried properly from the drizzle they'd encountered on Ben Nevis. She shivered a little.

A low rumbling noise emerged from under the tyres of the minibus as it crossed what must have been a cattle grid and shortly afterwards the vehicle slowed to a halt. The snoring stopped. Peter shifted and the rest of the bus stirred itself into life. Someone pulled open the sliding door and Monica saw with dismay that it was pelting with rain outside. With enormous reluctance she reached for her rucksack and stumbled outside. The guide Meade had recruited to get them up and down the three mountains, a bearded young man who went by the name of Rug, gathered them together in a group and offered a half-hearted pep talk. "All right, my hearties," he said. "All set for mountain number two? Scafell Pike's waiting up there for us to go and say hello."

Rug adjusted the head-torch which he had pulled over a thick woolly hat which in turn was pulled over his hair and did a quick head-count of the group. Long blond dreadlocks hung down the back of his neck. He'd already herded his flock safely off Ben Nevis but since then he had been at the steering-wheel of the minibus, tackling the Saturday afternoon traffic on the motorway south. Monica thought he looked tired. She also thought that he looked rather too much like her younger brother. This was a worrying thought: Sam, particularly when he was stoned, could be good company but you'd never dream of asking him to take you up a mountain in the middle of the night. Monica hoped Rug knew what he was doing.

One by one the party shouldered their rucksacks and stood there on the roadside waiting. The minibus was empty now except for Meade himself, still talking into his mobile. He covered it with his hand, and opened the window to address Rug. "You go on," he said. "I'll be off the phone in a minute or so and I'll catch you up. The first part of the path's easy to follow, and I've got my torch." He closed the window and recommenced his conversation. A gaggle of his wet and dispirited employees, along with an over-enthusiastic Rug, disappeared into the night.

2.

Nick Potterton woke to a buzzing close to his right ear. The mobile phone. He looked at the alarm clock over on the other side of his bed, which told him it was just after five in the morning.

At a time like this, there was only one explanation for the phone summoning him from sleep – a call-out. In around forty other homes in Nick's home village of Grasmere and around Ambleside his fellow mountain rescue team members would also have heard the same noise, would also be heaving themselves awake.

Nick jumped out of bed and found his reading glasses. As he expected, there was a short text message on the phone. A woman called Pat, the President of the local mountain rescue team who was also the current Team Leader, would have activated the automated software program which triggered the alert.

Nick heard driving rain at his upstairs bedroom window, thought briefly about crawling back to bed but instead texted a response: A15. 'A' was for affirmative – it meant he was volunteering. The rest of the message communicated that he should be at the mountain rescue base in no more than fifteen minutes.

All the kit he would need for a wet, and potentially long, foray on the fells was beside the bed, put there in anticipation of exactly this eventuality. No time to wash, of course. He pulled on the clothing, layer by layer, hurried down the stairs of his small cottage and put the car key in the ignition. About ten minutes later he was in Ambleside, drinking a coffee someone had thrust into his hands and chatting to the other team members who had already shown up.

It was Pat herself who led a short briefing. Cumbria police had rung just after half past four to ask for the team's support. A big search had been started over at Wasdale Head and although the local mountain rescue team along with two of the dogs and their handlers were already out, the police were anticipating that reinforcements from other search and rescue teams would be needed. A white male, in his forties, had become separated from his party somewhere on the slopes of Scafell Pike. The group had been attempting a charity Three Peaks event.

A slight sigh went round the room. The burgeoning interest in the challenge of climbing the highest mountains in Scotland, England

and Wales in one go was not particularly welcome with many local people and Lakeland mountain rescue teams had too often had to go out to shepherd inexperienced and ill-prepared parties of walkers safely back to their coaches or minibuses. Not that it made any difference to the way they approached their work: if there were people at risk on the mountains, they were there to try to help them.

Working as a mountain rescue team member wasn't how Nick earned his living. Like all the rest of the team, he was a volunteer. Professionally he was a journalist, once upon a time a high-flying London hack working for the Sunday Times on hard-hitting investigative stories and now, following the mid-life split-up with his long-time partner Ana and a retreat to the Lake District mountains, a fearless freelance contributing stories on school fetes and the like for the *Cumbrian Enquirer*. His career, he had to admit, had begun to look decidedly iffy. Still, he was making progress on a book he'd persuaded a gullible publisher to commission. *Nuclear Power: Yes Please?* just might give him the professional boost he badly needed. He'd promised the publisher a no-holds-barred expose of the way that commercial interests had been pushing a whole new generation of nuclear power plants, and although he was late with the deadline the book was actually coming together rather well.

The briefing was over and the team was making its way towards the garage where the 4x4 ambulances and the minibus were housed. Nick fell in step with Lindsay Maddens, a close friend who had joined Mountain Rescue at the same time as he had, eighteen months or so back. They'd both been shaken by the death of another member of their fellrunning club who had fallen and died during a fell race. Together they'd gone through the training courses and practices for the mountain rescue team, and together been admitted as full members earlier that year. Since then they had already been out with the team on several call-outs. They had helped stretcher a walker with a fractured leg off Seat Sandal, had dealt with an injured mountain biker on the bridleway in Far Easedale and had located a young couple who had got themselves lost somewhere near the summit of Red Screes when the mist had rolled in unexpectedly.

Now once again the call had come through that the mountain rescue team was needed. "Could be a long day," Nick said. "Could be," Lindsay agreed.

3.

It was the first time in her life Monica Roughlee had stayed in a youth hostel. 'Stay' was probably not the right verb to use in the circumstances.

The police had arranged it, knocking up the night warden of the Wasdale Hall hostel at some ridiculous time in the early hours of Sunday morning and telling her firmly to find space for a party of wet and distraught walkers who had just returned from the slopes of Scafell Pike. Monica found herself billeted in a cheerless dormitory with Raisha, with her office colleague Peggy and (was this appropriate?) with Peter as well. The warden had rustled up some bedding and blankets.

Peggy had initially tried to resist. "But we have to drive on to Snowdon," she'd told the policeman. "If we don't, we won't get our sponsorship money." The policeman had simply laughed, a bleak and uncaring laugh.

They were all there in the hostel, all except Rug who had last been seen sitting in a police car being asked questions by two policemen. And Mr Meade of course. Nobody knew where he was. Although Monica gathered that quite a lot of people were out on the mountain at this moment looking for him.

She'd managed a few hours' disturbed kip before being woken by the warden. "Half past nine," she'd said. "The police are waiting downstairs."

And indeed they were, two of them, one man and one woman, both looking far too young for the uniforms they were sporting. They'd announced that they would be taking statements from all the group, just a routine enquiry they'd said reassuringly. Nothing to worry about. But Monica had found it intimidating none the less.

The police had taken over the warden's private office, and now were sitting across a small table from her. It was the policewoman who asked the questions. First she'd wanted to know Monica's full name, and her date of birth and where she lived. Then the questions turned to the events of the previous night.

"When did you last see Richard Meade?" Monica had been asked.

"In the minibus, just before we started off to climb up Scafell Pike," she'd replied. "He was on the phone. He said he'd catch us up."

"Can you remember exactly what he said?"

"I think he said he'd only be a short time, and that he knew the first bit of the way."

"And then you started walking?"

"Yes. It was pitch black, but we'd all been told to bring head torches. Rug, he was the guide, he told us to stick together. We hadn't gone far before we had to stop. Raisha turned over her ankle on a rock, so we hung around for a bit until she said she was OK to carry on."

"No sign of Mr Meade yet?"

"No. No, he'd not caught us up."

"And you carried on?"

"Yes, Rug took us up a path. I've never been in rain like that before. It was just falling out of the sky and drenching us. I think I heard some thunder, too. It was just horrible."

"How long were you walking?"

"I don't know," Monica said. "I was soaked through. And it was freezing cold. It didn't feel like summer, it was like being in a winter wilderness on that mountain."

"You've no idea how long you were walking?"

"It felt like hours. My feet were really painful. Maybe it was only half an hour or so. Or less."

"And then?"

"Then we stopped, and Rug said we couldn't go on because the path divided and Mr Meade still hadn't arrived. We waited for a while and then Rug said we'd have to go back. People complained – well, everyone was thinking about how we had to complete the Three Peaks – but Rug said he'd vouch that we'd as good as climbed up Scafell Pike. And anyway it was pouring with rain and everyone was soaked right through, so in the end we were all pretty happy to turn back."

"Back to the minibus."

"Yes. And it was locked. And Mr Meade wasn't there. We must have missed him somewhere on the path."

"OK. He was your boss, wasn't he? Did he know the Lake District well, would you say? Was he an experienced hill-walker?"

"Maybe, but he'd never told us that he was. He had to buy all the kit for this trip, just like the rest of us."

The policewoman paused. "Well I'm sure we'll find him soon. We'll try to arrange for you to get back home soon, but for the time being the warden here has said you can use the lounge. She's going to light a fire. Better make yourself comfortable."

4.

Nick Potterton had settled into a rhythm, one foot in front of another, moving forward steadily but without rushing. He was on the western slope of Lingmell, one of Scafell Pike's neighbouring mountains, slowly making his way northwards. The weather had improved, and although the clag was still down the rain had eased and the sun seemed to be trying to break through. Nick didn't often come over to this part of the Lakes, so all in all and despite the early start he was enjoying being out on the fells. Lindsay Maddens was a short distance across from him, and strung out beyond her in a line were four others from mountain rescue, systematically quartering the ground. Just in case. Just in case there was a casualty ahead, waiting to be found.

There was really only one way to start out for Scafell Pike if you were a walker doing the Three Peaks and it would take you nowhere near where Nick now was. You'd park close by the National Trust campsite at the top end of Wast Water and then take the well-walked tourist path which follows the tumbling stream of Lingmell Gill up almost due eastwards. Then, unless for some reason you wanted to scramble up through Mickledore, you'd swing north-eastwards skirting an outcrop called Pikes Crag before turning back south-eastwards to make the final approach to the summit. It wasn't a classic walk and many walkers thought it a pretty dull affair but in the middle of the night it got you safely up and back. Well, normally safely.

The local Wasdale mountain rescue team, called out by the police almost immediately Richard Meade's absence had been notified to them by an anxious Rug, had focused their search on the land immediately adjacent to the tourist route up Scafell Pike, and then

– when nothing had come to light – had started widening the area to be searched to the whole of the western flanks of the mountain. The Ambleside team, having made the long journey over Hard Knott Pass, had been allocated Lingmell to the north. Frankly, this could be considered clutching at straws. Maybe, Nick thought to himself, someone could start out for Scafell Pike and end up on Lingmell but it wasn't an obvious mistake to make, even at night. Nevertheless, a man was missing and he needed to be found. He focused on the job in hand.

Down close to the National Trust campsite, the police had set up an impromptu control centre for the search in one of the Wasdale mountain rescue vehicles. In any mountain rescue situation, it is the police who call out the teams and who have ultimate control of the operation. This time a policewoman, Sergeant Chrissy Chambers, was in charge. Beside her was a large-scale map of Wasdale Head and the Scafell plateau, and beside the map was the volunteer who was leading the Wasdale team that day, a retired teacher called Bob Shakespear. Beside Bob in turn was another of the rescue team, acting as radio controller, calling up in turn each of the search teams on the fells to monitor their progress. In total, they had twelve teams of six out searching, together with four search dogs and their handlers.

"Time's getting on," Sergeant Chambers said. Shakespear nodded. He knew what she meant. It was now more than fifteen hours since this man Meade had gone missing. It had been a wet night and a cool day. Exposure – hypothermia – was highly likely to have set in.

Chambers knew something else, something she couldn't fully explain but which was causing her concern. When early that morning a police locksmith had come to open the minibus there inside at the front was a man's rucksack complete with waterproofs, a head torch and a pair of walking boots. The rucksack had the name Meade written in inside. It could mean that Meade had come well prepared, equipped not only with his own gear but with a complete set of spare kit just in case others needed it. Or it could mean that for some unknown reason Meade had chosen to set off to catch up with his party without even putting on his outdoor clothes or his boots. If so, the chances of finding him with any signs of life were increasingly remote.

"Reckon he ever set off? From the minibus, I mean." Shakespear was talking to her again, asking her something she had already considered several times. Because there was a third possibility. Had Meade, for who knew what reason, deliberately held back when the rest of his group had begun the climb towards Scafell Pike? Had he never intended to catch them up? Had he – somehow, in the middle of the night – managed to leave the remote valley of Wasdale without the minibus? Were the mountain rescue lads and lassies searching in vain for someone who was now safely ensconced in a Lake District pub with a pint of Jennings in his hand... or more likely was on a flight out of Manchester, doing a runner to somewhere like the Costa del Sol?

Chambers had, of course, not kept these thoughts to herself. During the day and at her request her police colleagues had been finding out what they could about Mr Richard Meade. He was 45 and living – so it transpired – in an altogether very pleasant residence on an upmarket estate a few miles out from Blackpool. Wrought iron railings and CCTV, and predictably no-one at home when a couple of uniformed constables from the Lancashire force had gone knocking. He was the owner of a caravan site called Greensleeves – or rather, not a caravan site, it wasn't one of those holiday places but what you had to call a residential park, a place with so-called mobile homes permanently fixed to the ground and permanent residents to occupy them too. Mainly older people, it seemed, who'd moved out from Preston or Blackburn or one of the Lancashire industrial towns when they had come to retire. The Greensleeves office was closed and nobody appeared to be on duty, Chambers learned: but then it was Sunday and all the remaining staff as far as she was aware were refugees in the Wasdale Hall youth hostel.

According to the interviews Chambers' police colleagues had conducted earlier in the day with Meade's staff, he was divorced, with two sons either side of twenty who were now living with their mother near Hull. No criminal record, although the police national computer showed up that an officer had been called a year or so back to Greensleeves when one of the residents, a man in his eighties, had barricaded himself in Meade's office, complaining about the bill he'd been sent for the sewers or something. The incident was put down by Lancashire Constabulary as caused by dementia. Sad how many older people were affected.

Basically, Chambers thought to herself, Meade was shaping up to be a Mr Anyone, one of the broad mass of the population who never come into contact with the police except perhaps for the odd motoring misdemeanour, who live their lives in their own way, make money, have children, presumably have fun, find themselves growing older. And who just occasionally, like Meade, have unfortunate accidents whilst doing things like walking in the fells at night to raise money for charity.

"The Ambleside guys will be getting tired," Shakespear commented. He had already organised replacement volunteers from his own Wasdale team who had taken over the main search after lunch. "Any reason not to stand them down soon?" Chambers shook her head. It would be light until after nine, but the search teams had now fanned out into countryside far away from the route that anyone in their right mind would have taken towards Scafell Pike. The dogs had found nothing, and a police helicopter which had also joined in the search from the sky had been sent away again after a couple of hours. It looked like being an abortive day.

It was true that Nick and his colleagues were ready for a break. He and his team had spent the day west of Lingmell, moving round the hillside broadly keeping between the 200 and 250 metre contours. They were now far from the summit of Scafell Pike, and a considerable distance from the National Trust campsite at Wasdale Head as well. They'd looked after themselves and each other, eating and drinking regularly, but they had also covered a considerable amount of ground. They'd found a dead sheep but nothing else of note. Ninety-nine per cent certain, Nick thought, that there is no casualty waiting to be found on these slopes.

He responded to a call from the search team leader, who signalled across to the other five in the team to make their way to join her. "Control has just radioed through," she said. "Nothing found, and they're going to stand us down. I suggest we drop down the fellside and follow Lingmell Beck back towards Wasdale Head. Everyone still all right?" Everyone nodded.

In any search there is always the desire to carry on. Just a few more metres may make all the difference. Just one more outcrop of rock might bring a sighting of the casualty. But Nick's mountain rescue team, though comprised as it was of volunteers, prided itself on being professional. The order had come through to finish the search. The team immediately turned for home.

They were a mile or so short of the National Trust campsite and Nick was chatting inconsequentially to Lindsay Maddens when the radio crackled into life again. It was control, calling all search teams. Nick's leader listened intensely, and then relayed the message to the group.

"Word has come through that two walkers have found a casualty. A delta casualty," she said.

Nick and Lindsay exchanged glances. As all mountain rescue members knew, this meant there was a casualty who would no longer be in need of any sort of medical care. D for Delta as in D for dead.

"Not yet clear that the casualty is the man we've been searching for, although initial indications are that it is," the leader went on. "White middle-aged male. Strange thing is, the walkers who found him were miles away, completely the other side of Wast Water. They were dropping down from Haycock. They found the casualty in a bog on the far side of Seatallan, in the Pots of Ashness."

"Pots of Ashness," Lindsay had said. "I don't think I know it."

"Wilderness country," Nick had replied. "Tussocks. Marshland. Not on the way to anywhere."

"Not on the way to Scafell Pike, anyway."

"No. What on earth was he doing over there?"

"Poor guy."

They walked back in silence.

5.

Hypothermia is the silent killer of the mountains, a Lake District shadow who can tag along as a companion even for experienced hill-walkers. Its technique is straightforward: it strikes when its victim gets cold and wet and doesn't do anything about it. Normally humans have a body temperature of around 37° centigrade but if this falls by a couple of degrees hypothermia sees its chance to get a grip. You'll start shivering, and you'll probably also lose concentration, so that you start taking silly navigational decisions. You'll probably start feeling bad-tempered, too. Watch out, hill-walkers are told, for the umbles: someone who begins grumbling, mumbling and stumbling is someone potentially seriously at risk.

And then, as the body temperature drops further, the shivering stops. The body gives up on extremities like the arms and legs and focuses on the core. Lips and fingers turn blue. The heart rate and breathing slows. Less oxygen is carried in the blood. Below about 32° there's no longer any energy being generated to keep the muscles working. You may lose consciousness. Or you may just decide that the best thing to do is to take a short kip. You never wake up, of course.

Richard Meade had been out in wild country on a filthy night. Hypothermia had probably set in quite quickly. Nature in the Lake District could be beautiful, as thousands of tourists taking their photographs of Windermere or Coniston Water or Grasmere knew very well. But nature could also be cruel. And sometimes nature could be given a helping hand, by people's own actions.

The impromptu police control centre had been shifted on Sunday evening from the vehicle borrowed from the mountain rescue guys to a proper police caravan, dragged up the valley road by a police 4x4 and plonked down on the grassy car park close to the top of Wasdale Head. Chrissy Chambers, feeling tired and sweaty inside her uniform after what had already been a long day was at the table inside the trailer but was no longer in charge. That role belonged to a detective chief inspector who had arrived at more or less the same time as the trailer. George Mulholland was old-school, the sort of policeman who you felt belonged in a past age of policing, a world which was somehow simpler and more kindly. Mulholland got results, though, as many a Cumbrian criminal knew to their cost. Beneath his avuncular manner was a cop who deserved respect. With Mulholland were a man and a woman, a detective sergeant and a detective constable, drafted in at short notice presumably to be Mulholland's gofers.

"Good evening," he looked around, "gentleman and ladies. Once again we find that members of the public don't want us to enjoy a pleasant weekend with our loved ones. Our lot is indeed not a happy one. Sergeant Chambers, tell us about this unfortunate incident."

"Yes, sir," she replied. "The casualty was found at approximately 1730 this afternoon by two walkers in an area of open moorland northwest of Wast Water. We have secured the scene, and forensics have been called. The doctor's already been and formally declared him dead. Photographer's on his way. We've also called for some floodlights to be taken up there. Access is only by a footpath and about a three mile walk, it's not easy. Two constables are there at the moment."

"And the body? Identification? Is it the misper you've been looking for?"

"Nothing firm yet of course, but, yes, it would appear to match the description of the Three Peaks walker who was reported missing. A Mr Richard Meade, a businessman."

"The body was found by two walkers. Is that right?"

"Yes, sir. We have taken statements. They were very shaken up. One of them had vomited at the scene. Unfortunate for the forensics, of course."

"And the walkers were, as you say, shaken. Because of the somewhat unusual appearance of the body?"

Chambers had briefed Mulholland informally on this aspect of the case when he had first arrived. He had said nothing at the time but his eyebrows had arched interrogatively.

"Yes, sir. The victim was on his front, with his face in a patch of sphagnum moss. He was shirtless and wearing just boxer shorts. Initial searches have failed to find any discarded clothing nearby but we're still looking."

"Cause of death?"

"The primary cause of death according to the doctor may well have been hypothermia. The weather was terrible all last night. All the usual steps were taken after the body was found to try to see if life could be brought back, but without effect. Obviously the pathologist is now investigating." She paused. "The PM when it comes back should tell us more."

"Sergeant Chambers, indulge me. I'm an old man and my brain is not as young or undoubtedly as fast as yours. Tell me why you think this man appears to be so singularly lacking in clothing."

"Sir, I suppose there are two explanations. One is suicide. It has happened before. Someone can't cope, walks off into the hills, carries on walking knowing they will never come back. Taking off your clothes would speed the inevitable. It would be pretty painless and quite quick, not a bad way to go."

"Suicide, yes, very plausible." Mulholland appeared to be weighing up her words. "Your second explanation?"

"Well, I'm not sure. Perhaps someone could in some way have forced him to take off his clothes or even done it themselves. Someone who also stopped him finding shelter or returning to safety."

"Hmm. A third party. Hastening him to a soggy if not completely watery grave." He stopped briefly. "Were such an event to have occurred, when would it have been?"

"Between the time his fellow walkers began to ascend Scafell Pike, which was about one o'clock this morning from what they've told us, and the time when his body was found. Probably during darkness, when the weather was at its worst."

"Mr Meade, if indeed that is the unfortunate gentleman, was last seen at Wasdale Head, am I right? And his body was found in a somewhat less well frequented part of our Cumbrian landscape called Ashpans?"

"Pots of Ashness, yes," Chambers replied. "Over four kilometres away, as the crow flies.

"Likely route?"

"I've thought about this, sir, and I don't have a ready explanation. There's a footpath from the edge of Wast Water towards the mountain called Haycock which goes somewhere close to the Pots of Ashness, but it starts a good mile or so down the road from where the minibus was parked. Alternatively, you'd have to climb all the way up Yewbarrow and then down the other side. That's a major undertaking. Or I suppose you could head north and then turn back across the col between Yewbarrow and Red Pike, but that's a very long way round and would still involve some serious clambering. All three routes are challenging."

"Thank you, Sergeant. Any background on Mr Meade?"

"He lived near Blackpool. We were in touch earlier with Lancashire Constabulary. This is what we know so far."

She passed papers across the table.

"Next of kin?"

"A divorced wife and two sons, aged 21 and 17. No current partner that we know of. I assume the sons are technically next of kin. Humberside somewhere. I'm not sure we have the address yet."

"Good." He turned to the plainclothes man beside him. "Patrick, follow this up, will you? We will need Lancashire on board. We may need to ask for someone down there to tag along with us. Pity to have to field another team's player, but needs must." He turned back to Chrissy Chambers.

"You have statements from the walkers who found him? Where are the walkers now?"

"One of my colleagues interviewed them. They are on a walking holiday and are staying at a B&B over in Eskdale. We have the details."

"Mr Meade's mountain guide? And his companions?"

"Statements from them too. The guide lives in Kendal and we sent him home. Goes by the name of Rug, although his name is Rupert Rugglesdon." She paused before continuing. "One of my constables did the interview and said something seemed not quite right. As if he was holding back on something."

"Perhaps just in shock?"

"Well, yes, perhaps. As for the other charity walkers we arranged for them to be billeted in the Wasdale Hall youth hostel. They were all interviewed this morning, when we were still dealing with a missing person of course." She stopped abruptly. "God, they'll still be there. Sorry, sir, I've just realised that I should have sorted out some transport to get them home. It's been a rather busy day."

"And it is set to be an even busier week ahead. Sergeant, I'm happy if you want to get home now, but it would be helpful to have you back tomorrow first thing. I'll speak to your superintendent and see what we can agree. I'll be working from the incident room in Whitehaven, by the way. We'll keep the trailer here as a field base."

Mulholland turned to the detective constable. "Susie, better sort out the youth hostellers. Tell them a body has been found but don't give details. If you can find transport to get them home tonight do so, although they may have to stay another night. Patrick," (this to the detective sergeant), "make sure the minibus is properly secured and guarded overnight. Oh and talk to our media people and get them to put out a press release. Just say that a body has been found near Wasdale which may be the missing walker. Nothing else. Nothing about his state of attire at this stage."

He spread his hands expansively. "Class dismissed. We few, we happy few, will assemble again tomorrow."

Monday

1.

Nick had planned to give himself a lie-in on Monday morning – there had to be some advantages of being self-employed – but his mobile phone had other ideas. Shortly after nine it began ringing, the irritating jazzy ring-tone which Nick had never liked but could never quite work out how to change.

The team had got back to the Ambleside mountain rescue base from Wasdale Head around seven the previous evening, had got the vehicles ready and waiting for a quick departure whenever the next emergency call came through, and had then had a short debrief. After that, he and Lindsay had found a pub. They were both physically tired and hungry, but the drink was a necessary part of unwinding and they enjoyed each other's company. As they both knew, the time when each of them had been getting over messy relationship break-ups and when they might have ended up as lovers had long passed. Lindsay now was happily into a new relationship with a cycling chartered surveyor called Phil from Carlisle, but of all the people Nick had got to know since moving north to Cumbria she remained one of his closest friends.

They talked briefly of the search but quickly moved on to talk of other things, of work, and holidays ahead, and Nick's daughter Rosa, and gossip from the fellrunning club they both belonged to. In mountain rescue, you couldn't afford to get too emotionally caught up. For your own sanity you had to keep a certain distance and sometimes try to forget what you'd witnessed.

Nick had got back to his home in Grasmere later that evening, had cracked a couple of eggs for an omelette and been in bed and asleep by eleven. And now it was Monday morning. Still not dressed, he reached for the phone.

"Hello?"

"Morning, Nick, not too early I hope? I'm looking for a freelance journalist with a nose for a good story who meets their deadlines without fail and who can do me 1200 words by Thursday," the voice said. "Oh, and who is prepared to accept a ridiculously low fee. I thought of you."

Nick had immediately identified the caller. He and Martin Eveyard had worked together many years back at the Sunday Times.

Those had been exciting times. Both of them were at the start of their journalistic careers, and both were fortunate to be working at a time when newspapers still had the time and the inclination to probe a little below the surface of the news. Inevitably, almost all the people he'd known at the Sunday Times had gone on to do different things. A couple of old colleagues had turned into academics, lecturing on journalism to a new generation of would-be hacks. Some had moved into PR, or out of the industry altogether. Martin was the exception: he had stayed in journalism and was now features editor at the Observer. Nick had kept in touch with him over the years, but only in a half-hearted way. To be honest, when he'd realised that the relationship with the one woman he'd loved with all his heart was over, when Ana had moved out of their shared home back to her native Catalonia and he'd taken the wilful decision to leave London and move about as far as you could go before you ran out of England, he'd also made the unconscious decision to let his London network of friends and contacts drop. It must have been at least a couple of years since Martin had last rung.

"Not sure I meet that person spec, Martin," Nick replied. "Not that last bit about the fee anyway. But what's the story?"

The story was all too topical. Sunday had been a relatively quiet news day, and the story of the missing Three Peaks charity walker in the Lakes had made it to the bottom half of some of the radio and TV news bulletins.

"I'm not particularly interested in the man who went missing," Martin went on. "Anyway I gather they've found his body now, so that story's dead and buried." Nick winced at the choice of words. "But I think there's something we could do on the whole Three Peaks phenomenon. I gather more and more people are doing it and I also understand not everyone's very pleased about this. Interested in taking this on? I'd need quotes from people who have done the challenge, people from the charity sector, some of the companies who organise the events, irate local neighbours and farmers, all the usual sort of stuff. For next Sunday, of course."

Nick thought quickly. His agreement with Molly Everett the editor of the *Cumbrian Enquirer,* the paper where he did informal freelance shifts a few times a week, didn't preclude him from taking on other commissions, and this wasn't an angle on the story which

Molly would have wanted. Anyway, work at the *Enquirer* was looking decidedly uncertain at the moment.

"Yes, that sounds do-able," Nick replied. "Let me put through a couple of calls before I definitely commit. I'll ring you straight back. So we just need to talk money." A good-natured bargaining session began. Freelance fees in journalism had fallen shockingly in recent years, but Nick had a shrewd idea how high he could push Martin. A deal was done.

There was in fact just one phone call Nick wanted to make. When he'd been recruited into mountain rescue, he'd made it clear that he wouldn't be writing up anything he participated in for the *Cumbrian Enquirer*: you couldn't be out on the fells as a mountain rescue volunteer and then once you got home turn it into a news story. But in this case, Nick felt, he wasn't being asked to write about the particular circumstances of yesterday's search and his mountain rescue experience wouldn't feature at all. Out of courtesy he rang Pat as the team's President and as he'd expected she told him to go ahead.

The lie-in long forgotten, Nick pondered his options. Mondays were normally ear-marked as *Yes Please?* days, ones which he dedicated to the book. The research was more or less completed and the writing-up was coming together nicely. He had around 70,000 words already done and was currently tackling one of the two remaining chapters, lifting the lid on the background to the proposed Hinkley Point nuclear reactor in Somerset which had been subject to so much governmental uncertainty in recent times. But yesterday's events, and Martin's call this morning, had somehow broken his routine. He decided instead to get to work straightaway on the feature.

Martin Eveyard was right: this was a good journalistic story. The idea of encouraging people to climb the highest points in Scotland, England and Wales had taken off in recent years, and there were some people who felt the whole thing had got out of hand. Those living close to the approach road to Wasdale Head, for example, often complained of excessive night-time traffic as groups who had done a daytime ascent of Ben Nevis jumped back in their coaches and minibuses and sped down the Scottish roads to Cumbria to arrive to tick off Scafell Pike before dawn. Some groups seemed hopelessly ill-prepared for what they were tackling. Sometimes it seemed that parties of walkers expected that the path up to the top of England's highest mountain would be tarmaced all the way with lights every ten yards.

Of course, there were good things about these Three Peaks events too, and not just that they raised money for charity. Encouraging people from city areas to get to know Britain's mountains had to be a good thing... didn't it? There was that sense of achievement to be had from completing a challenge involving ten thousand feet of ascent and descent. Didn't the NHS want people to be more active and more healthy?

And, anyway, wasn't the great thing about the mountains and moors the fact that they were open to all without hindrance? In a consumerist society, here was one thing which still hadn't succumbed to the urge to turn everything into a commodity. The mountains were there, freely available for all to enjoy.

Although, Nick Potterton thought to himself, actually the whole Three Peaks thing was now very much something which had been packaged up ready to be purchased. Several private companies were engaged in selling their services in arranging Three Peaks challenge events, for profit of course. Book a group trip for ten or a dozen people and you'd probably have to fork out two or three thousand pounds for the experience. It meant you had to raise even more for your favourite charity before you even got into the black.

Some of these firms were trying hard to be reputable, Nick accepted. There'd been a move in recent years by some of them to discourage the idea of doing the challenge within a 24 hour deadline, a practice which had led to night-time traffic in the Lakes and had probably made things more dangerous too. But nevertheless the Three Peaks challenge had become controversial. Nick knew he had been given a commission for a story which he'd be able to really enjoy tackling.

He looked out at the window, and saw that the weather had changed. The sun was shining. He reached for the car keys.

2.

Polly Prescott was stripping the bedding from the dormitory bunks when she heard hammering at the hostel door. She ignored it. It was after ten in the morning, which meant that all the hostellers were gone for another day and she was able to get to grips with the chores. She'd be opening the front door again at five, but until then any would-be hostellers would have to disappear up a mountain or, perhaps, amuse themselves in the Wasdale Head Inn.

She was ready for a break. Yesterday had been exceptionally difficult. Of course she'd been happy to take in a marooned party of Three Peaks walkers, even if the knock-up from the police had come at some ungodly time in the small hours. The hostel had been busy on Saturday night but she'd just about had enough beds for the group, even if she'd had to break the usual rules and billet men and women in the same dorms. Well, it was an emergency.

But her surprise visitors began to outstay their welcome. The police had been back on Sunday after breakfast, a couple of young officers who took an interminable time taking down statements. Before they'd finished it was already lunchtime so she gave the party an impromptu packed lunch which they ate in front of the log fire in the living room. And then the police, just as they were eventually leaving, had told her guests that they had to stay put in the youth hostel. Polly was left in charge of a party who were fed up with the jigsaws and games of Ludo the hostel could offer and who were desperate to get home. What's more, they appeared to consider it a deliberate slight that that their mobile phones were unable to pick up signals.

"Two choices," Polly had told one of the group, a young woman called Raisha. If you walk up there" – Polly pointed out of the window at the ring of mountains which enclosed Wast Water – "you'll get the signal fine. Alternatively you ask me nicely and I let you use the landline."

So one after the other they'd lined up and made their calls home. And then Polly had had to deal with the aftermath. One of the other women was almost in tears. "The bastard never asked how I was. He never asked about me at all. All he said was that we'd failed to get round the Three Peaks and that he'd want his £10 sponsorship back."

She snivelled into a hanky. Polly supplied her with a weak cup of tea, two sugars, and two of her own paracetamol.

And then, eventually, just as it looked as if she would be hosting the house party from hell for a second night, they were gone. The police had come back, more phone calls had been made and cars had been summoned from spouses and partners. Polly waved them off and then got on with her proper job, looking after all the other hostellers she was accommodating that evening.

All in all, it was a relief to shut up shop at ten that morning and get on with the domestic duties. She was carrying the bag of dirty laundry downstairs when she heard the hammering again. Somebody was keen. Damn, she suddenly thought, it must be the police once more. She hurried down to the front door, pulled back the bolts and opened it.

"Polly," said the visitor. "I'm really sorry. I know you're closed."

It was a man who she knew was called Nick. She'd met him a few times at fellrunning events, didn't know him particularly well but did know that he was a good friend of Lindsay Maddens. Lindsay and Polly both did triathlons and often socialised in the time they had off work.

"Come in," she said.

"You need to know first why I'm here. I am wearing an invisible felt hat with a ribbon round it, and tucked in the ribbon is a card marked 'press'," Nick responded.

Of course, Polly remembered now, his name was Nick Potterton and as well as being a runner and a friend of Lindsay's he was a journalist with the *Cumbrian Enquirer.*

"Whatever your question my answer is 'no comment'," she'd replied, but smiling. "Or at least I might be prepared to blab to a journalist, but only if you undertake to put through all the washing and give the dormitories a decent vac first."

"Lovely. I appreciate the help I get in my job from the public," he'd said.

Polly led him into her private kitchen and put on the kettle. "Here about yesterday's incident?" she asked.

"Indirectly, yes. By the way, you know Lindsay and I were over here yesterday? My search and rescue team was called out to help. Apparently we were looking in all the wrong places, though."

He sipped at the coffee he'd been proffered and explained the feature he had been commissioned to write.

"I'm not looking to put you on the spot but I thought you'd know people in the valley who feel strongly about the whole Three Peaks business. One or two neighbours who might give me a quote," Nick said.

She thought for a moment. "You could talk to a couple of people I know down in Nether Wasdale," she replied. "They've both been vociferous about the problems. All the night-time noise, and the lights from the vehicles coming through their windows, and the general state of the footpaths after the season is over, the litter and the erosion issues and so on. These are locals who are not anti-tourist by any means, but who really don't want the Three Peaks walkers here." She paused briefly. "I'd gladly tell you what I think, too, but it would have to be off the record. You'd need to talk to the YHA media people for something official. But, you know, you're about twelve hours too late. The birds have all flown." She explained briefly her unexpectedly full house.

"Story of my life, another scoop missed," Nick replied. "I don't suppose you have their names and addresses?" he went on, apparently casually.

"I can't give personal info about hostellers," she said.

"No, of course not." He paused. "Although I suppose the question technically is whether they were hostellers or just some waifs you took in off the hills? Did they flourish their youth hostel membership cards at you, or whatever you have these days, and pay their way?"

He had picked on a sore point. "Since you ask, no, and I've no idea whether I'll ever get any money from them," she had replied. "I've got their details, of course, but given the unusual circumstances I didn't process them in the official register. I suppose..." She tailed off and looked across the room.

Nick followed her gaze and saw a pile of papers on the other side of the kitchen. They looked at each other. "Any chance you could pop out of the kitchen to get me one of those flapjack bars you've got on sale in the hostel shop?" Nick said. She pondered and then smiled and did as he suggested. When she returned, he was standing, ready to leave.

"Sorry, Polly, forgive me if I don't do the vacuuming today. Dust allergy." She laughed.

The door shut behind him and the hostel was once again firmly barred. Nick returned to his car. The story for Martin Eveyard was off to a better start than he'd dreamed possible. Nick now had the names and addresses for the local people he intended to call on before he left the valley that morning. More than that, he had acquired some other useful contact details. A trip down the M6 towards Blackpool was beckoning for later in the day. But first things first. Before he checked out any of Polly's leads he decided he would make time for himself. He might have been a desk-bound hack in those days in London when he was working at the Sunday Times but these days he was a Cumbrian fellrunner, and not a bad one either. How could he find himself in Wasdale and not go out for at least a short run? The running kit was as ever waiting in the boot of the car.

It was a whim, but he already knew where he intended to go.

Nick parked on the shore of Wast Water, quickly changed into a thermal top and his running shorts, pulled on his fell shoes and stuffed a waterproof, compass and map into a bumbag. He took a footpath he'd never explored before, a steady but frankly dull climb up a river valley which initially passed upland farmland before the mountains began to close in. Haycock was ahead, Yewbarrow was somewhere on his right, Seatallan out of sight to his left. Three miles or more ahead of him lay a patch of nondescript marshy ground with an intriguing name. There and back would take about an hour if he didn't dawdle, he'd decided.

He never got as far as he'd planned. Twenty or so minutes in, as he turned a corner in the path, he was suddenly aware that he did not have the fells to himself. Ahead he could see two figures moving about, both dressed in all-in-white protective bodysuits. Closer to hand was the unlikely sight of a police officer in full uniform.

The policeman hurried over towards Nick. "Sorry, sir, the footpath is closed today," he said. Nick noticed a flimsy patch of blue and white tape loosely draped across the path between two low shrubs. "You will have to turn back."

Nick tried his best. "That's all right, officer, I'm only following the footpath a short way further," he said, making as if to pass over the tape.

"No, sir. This is a crime scene. You can't proceed."

"Crime scene?" Nick was suddenly interested. "There was something on the news this morning about a missing walker's body being found. That's not a crime surely?"

The policeman ignored his question. "I'm afraid I must ask you again to turn back, sir." And then a question of his own: "Could you tell me why you have come here today?"

Nick thought quickly. Was he a fellrunner getting in some weekday training or was he a journalist? Both answers would be truthful. "Nick Potterton, I'm a journalist with the *Cumbrian Enquirer*. Your force issued a press release last night," he replied after a moment.

Nick noticed his name going down in the notebook which the policeman had pulled out. "Can you identify yourself?" the man asked. He was young but was already steeped in the need to do everything by the book, Nick thought.

"My NUJ Press Card is back in my car. But perhaps I could have a word with your superior officer?" he tried.

"No, you will need to talk to our media office. I'm sure they will be only too pleased to help."

Nick accepted defeat. But as he jogged back to his car he mulled over what the day so far had taught him. Sometimes, even now in his self-imposed semi-retirement from journalism, he still got the old thrill of the chase. Sometimes, he thought to himself, I still love my job.

3.

The grass which made up the landscaped areas between the individual mobile homes at Greensleeves residential park wouldn't stop growing. Jack Higgins hated it. He had waged his own very personal war against it for years, spending more of his working life than he cared to think about trundling backwards and forwards on the sit-down lawn mower.

But the bloody grass had grown again. His first task, he knew, when he got to work after the weekend would be to get the mower out and give the grass hell.

Alone of the seven employees who worked for Richard Meade at Greensleeves he had managed to get out of the Three Peaks caper. Dodgy knee, he'd told Meade. You'd find me too much of a liability, he'd said.

The price he would pay, apart from the opprobrium that had already come his way for not caring enough about the children's hospice, would be to have to listen to all the accounts of the weekend's adventures when the rest of the staff turned up. He knew immediately what they would say. Peggy would talk about how beautiful it had all been. Raisha would complain of being travel sick or maybe having a migraine. Peter would be full of himself and already claiming to be planning to tackle Everest next time. Monica would probably be the only honest one among them all, telling him that she hated the whole experience. And, as always with Monica, she would go on and on all about it at great length.

But at nine o'clock none of the office staff had arrived. The door stayed resolutely closed, much to the annoyance of some of the residents who were waiting there impatiently at opening time. They were wittering about how the overnight rain at the weekend had caused the drains to flood and their toilets to back up. How could one residential site, Jack asked himself, contain quite so many grumpy old men and grumpy old women?

In reality the drain problem was his responsibility as Greensleeves' all-purpose handyman, but Jack Higgins wasn't minded to short-cut the usual office procedures which had to be followed on occasions like this. Besides, he had several times told Meade that the whole drainage and sewage system needed complete modernisation. Meade, tight bastard that he was, had told him to make do. That was the way Meade ran the place: charge the poor buggers as much as you can, spend as little as possible in exchange, and live it up as often as possible in the golf club bar or wherever else it was he went.

Monica was the first of the office staff to arrive, sometime after half past nine, and all too soon Jack heard the story of the aborted Three Peaks challenge. Monica was in tears.

"The police told us they'd found a body," she sobbed as she entered the site, before she had even reached the office. "They wouldn't tell us whether it was Mr Meade so maybe it was somebody else. Maybe Mr Meade is safe somewhere. But why did he vanish like that? We just left him for a brief moment in the minibus and the next we knew he wasn't there."

She paused just for the time it took to pull out a paper hanky.

"They made us stay in this horrible dormitory. And then the police asked us lots of questions."

Another pause, before she continued. "Suppose he is dead? What shall we do? Who will pay us this month? I need the money, I can't survive without it."

Higgins shrugged. Peggy had by this time arrived too and had come over all motherly towards Monica. Eventually she put a scribbled note on the locked door to say that the office was temporarily closed. Inside she and Monica, and Raisha and two of the other admin staff when they finally showed up, could be seen moping about. Outside the office door the Grumpies were turning grumpier by the minute. Higgins made his way to the one part of the site which was his and his alone, the storeroom where the mower and all the other equipment was kept and which he had turned into his sanctum. Mowing could wait, he decided. Monica's words had affected him too: his position was different from hers, but he also was tied to Richard Meade for the money he needed to live on.

The day went from bad to worse. The man in the jacket and cord trousers showed up some time after lunch. Higgins knew immediately that he was a journalist. He had watched him from a distance as he had parked just outside the site, seen him somehow wangle his way into the office and had then watched him as he strolled around outside, talking to some of the residents. Higgins' first thought had been to confront the man and get him off the property but then decided not to bother. Meade could worry about all this – if, that is, Meade was still in a position to worry about anything.

But when the journalist came to find him in his own storeroom, Higgins decided enough was enough. He wasn't minded to play the man's little game. The exchange had been short.

"It's Jack Higgins, isn't it? I'm Nick Potterton, here for the Observer. They tell me in the office that you weren't with them for the Three Peaks trip this weekend?"

Higgins had grunted a reply.

"Can I ask, was there a reason why you didn't want to do the Three Peaks?" the man had persevered.

"May have been," Higgins had responded.

"Perhaps you don't particularly like walking in the hills?"

A further grunt had been the answer. The journalist had persevered.

"I'm sorry, I do know what a difficult day this is for everyone. I suppose I was simply wondering what you think about this way of raising money for good causes."

"None of your business what I think," Higgins had offered back.

"No, of course not." A change of tack. "Of course we don't know yet if the casualty found in the hills is Mr Meade, but I'm right, aren't I, that Mr Meade was a lifelong supporter of charities."

"So he claimed," Higgins had replied.

Potterton had paused at this. "He'd be sorely missed by the staff here at Greensleeves, wouldn't he?"

"By some people maybe." A pause, just time for an angry gesture. "Time for you to pack up your little notebook, whatever your name is. Off you go." Higgins had turned back ostentatiously to the rack of tools behind him and had picked up a heavy lump hammer. He was pleased to see the journalist blanch slightly and back his way out of the door. He'd thought of flinging the hammer at the retreating man, but immediately decided that a court case for GBH or worse wasn't really what he wanted just at the moment. Meade's death, if dead he was, was enough for one week.

4.

Molly Everett was having a lousy day. Her responsibility was to fill her newspaper each week with all the local news fit to print in time to send it off to the presses every Wednesday tea-time. It was Monday already, and instead of getting on with the job she had just been forced to have a two-hour meeting at the accountants. She took a puff on the electronic cigarette she hated so much and checked the messages which had come in while she'd been away.

Molly Everett was the editor of the *Cumbrian Enquirer*, the venerable local paper which had been a part of local life for what seemed like forever. Look in the paper's archive and – so the story had it – you'd probably find a report of the time Samuel Taylor Coleridge nearly came a cropper on Broad Stand trying to find a way off Scafell. Since then, the paper had chronicled Lake District life in war and peace, good times and bad. You felt that the *Enquirer* was just the sort of outstanding example of human cultural achievement that UNESCO really should be awarding with world heritage status.

But so what? A newspaper lives not on its past achievements but on its immediate future. And for the *Cumbrian Enquirer* the future was not looking good at all.

Everett had been found a seat in the small drab office in the accountancy firm where John Wythenshawe worked. Alongside her at the table were John Greet and Teresa Perkins, brother and sister, who between them were the holders of 80% of the *Enquirer*'s shares which they had inherited some years back from their father. Molly herself had the remaining minority shareholding, having been persuaded more than ten years back to invest some of her savings in the business which gave her her job.

Wythenshawe went through the latest accounts and pulled no punches. The *Enquirer* was in dire straits. Property advertising, once the staple of every local paper, had haemorrhaged away to the internet. Job adverts had gone the same way. And hardly anyone these days used the *Enquirer* small ads to sell their second-hand wardrobe or child's first bike.

Like every other paper the *Enquirer* had tried to compensate by moving online, but here too, despite all the effort which went into keeping the website updated, the revenue was simply not coming in. The business model which for several generations had provided communities up and down the country with local newspapers staffed by qualified journalists who could keep tabs on local politicians, report court cases and send photographers to every school fete and agricultural show had broken down.

"You lost fifteen thousand pounds in the first six months," John Wythenshawe said. "At this rate, your reserves will have gone by the year end. Frankly your fixed assets are next to worthless. The landlord's got a rent review on your office lease due next year, too. The only thing worth much at all is your brand, or in other words the *Cumbrian Enquirer*'s reputation."

Molly stayed silent for most of the meeting. Greet and Perkins, as effectively the owners of the title, discussed the options with their accountant. There was a possibility, it seemed, that one of the big newspaper groups might be prepared to take them over, probably for very little money and mainly just to acquire the title. If so, the new owners would almost certainly merge the *Enquirer* with its own existing Carlisle-based newspaper. But if not the paper would probably have to close at Christmas. They talked of drastic measures. Molly was told to cut back on her freelance budget and to try to persuade two of the older sports journalists to take early retirement. They'd keep the copy content up, they decided, by bringing in a couple of unqualified trainees in their place. And Molly was given the task of persuading the paper's readers to turn themselves into 'citizen journalists', sending in their own articles and photos for nothing.

Frankly after a meeting like that, Molly didn't know why she was bothering with this week's paper at all. But she couldn't help herself. She loved journalism, and she knew she was good at it. And just that morning a phone call had come in which she thought could be the basis of the front page lead.

It was the woman owner of a guest house over in Eskdale who had rung in. As well as cooking the breakfasts and doing all the usual B&B stuff she was a skilled craftswoman, and Molly had featured her and the contemporary knitwear she designed some months earlier in the paper. The feature had clearly gone down well, and now was pay-back time. Molly's hand moved effortlessly across her notepad shaping the Teeline shorthand letters as the woman told her story. Two of her guests had found a man's body while out walking at the weekend, Molly was told. They'd been so shaken up they'd had to talk to her about it. And what they couldn't get over was that the man had been almost completely naked. What did the *Enquirer* know about it all?

Molly didn't admit it but at that stage the *Enquirer* knew almost nothing – only the short press release which the Cumbrian police had put out late the previous night saying that a body had been found somewhere over by Wast Water. Walkers did have accidents and die in the hills, unfortunately, and usually their deaths were the basis for short news stories on the inside pages. This suddenly sounded rather more interesting.

This was, she felt, one of those occasions when it would be appropriate to flirt with George Mulholland. She and George had been at school together in Cockermouth and once when they were fifteen or so had shared a kiss on the way back from a party. The kiss was as far as it had gone. Shortly afterwards Molly had left school to become a junior reporter on the *Enquirer* and George had started out in the police as a wet-behind-the-ears police constable. Now he was in the CID, recently promoted to become a Detective Chief Inspector and she was the *Enquirer's* Editor. Long since they had both got married to their respective partners. Their relationship these days was a different one, based primarily on mutual self-interest. It is always useful for journalists to have friends in the police force they can talk to informally now and again, and Molly knew she had also in turn been able to be of help to George in his own work. Anyway what was wrong with a good flirt?

But when Molly Everett phoned Mulholland, having tracked him down in the Whitehaven police station where he seemed to be currently based, he was strangely unforthcoming. Of course, the bonhomie was still there, and in spades. "Molly," he said, "my long-lost love. How is the smell of hot metal these days?"

"George, you know very well we use litho presses. Stop pretending you're some old fart stuck in the 1950s wearing a tweedy jacket with leather patches. Nobody's taken in by your act, you know."

"But I have my faithful tweed jacket on as we speak," he responded. "Tell me, why the pleasure of your call?"

"How about the prospect of a pint of Jennings later today?"

It was the usual offer, and it usually brought the desired response. But not today. Mulholland brushed the offer aside.

"A delightful idea as always, and even more delightful if the company is to be you. But sadly not today. There are miscreants in

Cumbria who require my attention. Another time, most certainly, and I will buy the round."

Molly was forced to be more direct.

"Ah yes, the press release. The walker," Mulholland replied.

"George, I know that the body was pretty well naked when it was found. The police release didn't mention that. So what's this all about?"

There was a pause at the other end of the phone. "Molly, you must give up journalism and join the CID. Your sleuthing skills are what we need. But let me tell you that you will be the first person I will contact when we have anything more to tell you. Keep some space in your diary for a press conference very soon."

"Before my Wednesday press deadline?"

"Ah, well, that I can't say for sure. But soon, I'm sure." The call ended. Molly's pen tracked across the notepad. She had doodled a large black question mark on the page.

5.

For the second evening running, Nick was late home and obliged to throw together a scratch meal. He found some tortellini in the freezer and put on a pan of water. Then he took a pasta sauce jar from the store cupboard. There was some parmesan he could grate when the pasta was ready.

There were benefits to being single, he supposed, but they didn't include mealtimes. It was just too easy not to care too much when you were eating alone. The supermarkets didn't make it straightforward for you either, selling so much of their stuff in pre-packed quantities which were designed for couples if not for whole families. He knew he was letting standards slip. He told himself that maybe he should make an effort next weekend, have Lindsay and her bloke round for a proper meal perhaps.

Nick hated to admit it, but he had grown used to having just his own company. Ana was the gorgeously beautiful journalist with long dark hair who had been working at the time for the London desk of El País when she had captured his heart, who had shared the best part of two decades of his life but then six years or so back had walked out on him. She'd told him that she'd waited until their daughter Rosa had got through A levels and had got an offer of a place at Warwick but that she now wanted a new life for herself. She'd moved from London back to Catalonia, taken up a posting at one of Barcelona's daily papers and taken up with a new man as well. Jordi.

It had been a painful separation, for him if not for Ana, and he only generally heard news of her these days through Rosa. Rosa told him that she loved both her parents dearly and visited both the Lake District and Barcelona as often as she could but she was busy with her own career, working as a junior lawyer specialising in international commercial contract law. And she had her own life with her partner Becky. Rosa and Becky had met in their first week of university at Warwick and had immediately fallen in love. Their wedding had been the previous summer, in a rather nice Georgian mansion somewhere near Hampstead Heath.

Ana had been at the wedding of course. She looked older than she had been when Nick and she had first made love together in his old flat in Hackney, her naked body curled out across his bed and her black hair tumbling over her breasts, but in Nick's eyes she still looked quite stunning. Jordi was at the wedding too. Nick forced himself to be civil to them both and succeeded. It was after all Rosa's and Becky's big day. But at the wedding more than at any time since the separation he felt the isolation which came of being alone. He'd half thought of asking Lindsay to accompany him, but really that would have been an unreasonable demand on their friendship.

No, the few attempts he'd made to find a partner over the past few years had all petered out and, just for the moment a least, he would have to be happy with eating pasta for one. By and large, he decided, he was content with his life. He thought back over the previous few hours and felt the satisfaction of doing a good day's work.

He was much further on with the article for Martin Eveyard than he'd expected at this stage. He'd got the interviews with the unhappy locals in Wasdale sewn up and he'd also got some ideal quotes from his trip down to the residential park outside Blackpool. The visit to Greensleeves (who thought of these dreadful names?) had been far more productive than he'd expected. The young woman Raisa had been good value. "Gutted that we couldn't finish the Three Peaks," she'd said, in a Lancashire accent. "After all, we weren't doing it for ourselves, we were doing it for the kiddies at the hospice." And then there was the woman called Monica. Monica was unforgettable. She was as eager to please as a young puppy, a character trait she demonstrated by almost incessant chattering. She was also easily distracted. When Nick had asked her what she had thought of the Three Peaks challenge she'd talked to him about almost nothing except the state of her blisters.

But all in all Greensleeves staff had delivered what he needed. As he often did, he was playing around in his head with the possible opening paragraph. Something like this perhaps:

> Lancashire businessman Richard Meade died last Sunday
> morning on a Lake District hillside half-way through
> an attempt at the Three Peaks challenge. What had been
> planned as a way to raise much-needed funds for his local
> children's hospice went terribly wrong. But there are some
> in the outdoor world who feel that Mr Meade should not
> have even been in the Lake District last weekend. The idea
> of taking groups up and down Ben Nevis, Scafell Pike and
> Snowdon in one trip should be discouraged or perhaps even
> banned, they say.

Yes, the story was shaping up well. There were still calls he needed to make, of course. He needed to talk to the Institute of Fundraising who had devised a code of practice for Three Peaks challenges, and he also wanted to talk to some of the firms in the business of organising the trips.

That was the one disappointment of the day. He'd hoped to get Rug's side of the story, having heard all about the young man's enthusiastic approach to climbing mountains from several of the Greensleeves staff. Rug wasn't hard to find: a few Google searches on his smartphone led Nick to an old press article about a Duke of Edinburgh's Award leader who lived in Kendal who answered to the names of both Rug and Rupert Rugglesdon. There was an R. Rugglesdon in Kendal on BT's phone directory website, which helpfully gave Nick not only the address but also the map of how to get there. Nick diverted slightly on his way back home from

Greensleeves. It was early evening and when he arrived at a small terraced house near the town centre the lights were on.

The door had opened slightly to reveal a beard and, behind it, an expression of unease.

"It's Rug, isn't it," Nick had begun. "Nick Potterton, for the Observer. I'm writing a feature piece on the Three Peaks challenge and talking to experienced guides who lead groups. Is this a good moment to take a couple of minutes of your time?"

The knack on an occasion like this, as Nick very well knew, was to get invited in off the doorstep. But Nick had been out of luck.

"Sorry. I've nothing to say." The beard had wobbled slightly in reply.

"Well, as you know some people are rather critical of the whole Three Peaks idea, but I'm keen to get other people's opinions too. I hoped you'd be able to offer the contrasting viewpoint," Nick had persevered.

"No, you'd better talk to somebody else."

A last effort: "I've spoken to several people you've led in the past on Three Peaks challenges and they've spoken very highly of you."

"You're wrong. I haven't led Three Peaks challenges. Well, only one. And I've got nothing to say about that. Sorry, you've wasted a journey." Rug had firmly closed the door.

Nick had returned to his car wondering if he was losing his journalistic touch as he grew older. The time had been when he'd prided himself on his door-stepping technique. Oh well, if Rug wouldn't provide the quotes he needed he'd find others who would.

6.

George Mulholland took a bite from the flabby pizza one of the DCs had been out to get him and took stock of his day.

The pizza had arrived about twenty minutes back and had been waiting for him to notice it. A bottle of cola had been left for him as well. He took a sip. It was, he couldn't help reflecting, a poor substitute for the pint of Cumberland Ale that Molly Everett had offered him, but he told himself that duty was calling. Although it wasn't just a question of duty. Mulholland took pleasure from his work, loved in particular the intellectual satisfaction which came from piecing all the evidence together and cracking the puzzle. A successful prosecution later on against the guilty party – whoever they might be – was the icing on the cake, but it was the chase itself which got him fired up.

The evidence for his current enquiry was already coming in, but the conclusion was just at the moment proving elusive. Mulholland went through what he already knew, systematically.

The corpse found up on the fells was that of Richard Meade, of that Mulholland had no doubt. Mulholland had visited the body in situ before it had been transferred down to Wasdale late in the afternoon and taken by ambulance to a morgue. Plenty of photographs of Meade had been forthcoming via Google Images, most of them from local newspaper archives showing him handing over giant presentation cheques at some local Rotary function or other, and it was quite clear that this was the same man who had met his end at the Pots of Ashness. Formal identification by Meade's ex-wife was due to take place tomorrow. The woman had been visited by Humberside Police earlier in the day and had reluctantly agreed to the task. One of her sons was coming too, apparently. Mulholland planned to accompany them on the visit. There was still a great deal more he wanted to know about Meade's family background and this was an opportunity not to waste.

The police officers at the scene – Mulholland was careful not yet to think of it as a murder scene – had done their job assiduously. Unfortunately, there was as yet very little material coming through on the forensics side, but there had been something of a break-through in another respect. Two young officers had spent a tough day quartering the fells between Wasdale and the Pots of Ashness. A mile or so from the body they had found both a pair of men's trousers and a little further on, half-hidden under a rock, a waterproof jacket. These were now being carefully examined. Of course, they hadn't yet been linked to Meade but it was a fair guess that they would be. There was still no sign, though, of any kind of shirt, or of a torch. The searches would continue tomorrow.

Mulholland tried to picture the early hours of Sunday morning. It is lashing down, and pitch black. Meade takes off the jacket and his trousers. The question is, why? Is it willingly? Is there someone with him on the fells who gives him no choice, a shadowy figure or figures. A gun? A knife? A man, let's say, who is yelling at Meade against the wind: "Take your clothes off, or I shoot." The scenario seemed ridiculous.

So perhaps Meade is drugged. Mulholland thought back to those cases he'd tackled which involved what the media liked to call date rape drugs. Of course it was misleading to think that the only motive for using these drugs was for sexual assault. There were several drugs which could be used and they worked fast, particularly if alcohol had been consumed as well: fifteen minutes or half an hour could be enough to leave a victim unaware of what was happening to them.

The toxicology report from forensics, which Mulholland was hoping might be with him within the next twenty-four hours, might clear this up. Unfortunately some of these drugs were detectable only for a relatively short time, and Meade's body had been lying in the wilds for many hours before it had been discovered. Still, a positive test result would be the first firm evidence of foul play.

The fact was that Mulholland still didn't know for sure whether he was leading a murder investigation or simply convening an enquiry into the case of a bedraggled and benighted rambler who had come to grief in the hills. Just at the moment it suited him to tell the public that it was the latter. If there was someone out there with a hand in Meade's death it wouldn't hurt to leave them thinking that the police didn't suspect anything untoward. Still, trust Molly Everett to know more than she was supposed to. How had she known about Meade's lack of clothes? Mulholland suspected that her sidekick, that journalist Nick Potterton, had had a hand in this. He'd already had a report through from a junior officer that Potterton has been sniffing around up at the scene where the body was found.

Mulholland took another slice of cold pizza. Perhaps, after all, the clothes had been willingly taken off. A strange sexual encounter. Human beings could be both creative and quite incorrigible when it came to sex. Some people might get off on being semi-naked in the middle of the night in a bog in a rain storm. Mulholland pondered this and decided he wouldn't try it out himself.

In any case forensics had already reported that there was no sign of any sexual interference or other form of violence against the body. Meade's boxer shorts had been found in situ, exactly where they should have been.

Mulholland turned to other matters. The mobile phone. One of the interviews with the party in the youth hostel had mentioned that Meade had been on his phone during much of the journey towards the Lake District, and Mulholland had already put Chrissie Chambers on to contacting the network operator. What had come back had been the list of numbers called. Chambers was set to follow these up tomorrow and see what they revealed. Curiously, there were no calls recorded as being made by Meade after about 11.30pm on the Saturday night. So the call Meade was making at Wasdale Head which, according to the interviewees stopped him from starting up Scafell Pike, must have been made using a completely separate handset or at least a different SIM card. At present the police had failed to find one mobile belonging to Meade, let alone two.

Then there was Meade's Twitter account. He had been tweeting several times from his phone on the road down from Scotland. It was classic Twitter material: "Burger and chips near Gretna Green. Extra energy to tackle second of @TheThreePeaks" read one. "Workers at @GreensleevesResPark set to raise thousands £££ for children's #hospice. Scafell Pike next" read another. "Due Wasdale Head on our @TheThreePeaks challenge about 1am. Can't wait."

Mulholland didn't use Twitter himself and Meade's postings reinforced his view that this whole social media business was completely self-indulgent. But he didn't dismiss it. Twitter was turning out to be a valuable new tool. He had told two of his young detective constables to trawl through Meade's account, look at all his postings, check who he was following and who was following him. "And Facebook too. And do the same for whatever else you young people use these days. Tell me when you find anything interesting or surprising," he added. The DCs were in heaven: official authority to spend their work time messing about on social media, indoors, in the dry with plenty of coffee and biscuits. What was not to like about being in the CID?

It was getting late, already after nine o'clock. Mulholland knew he needed to get home if he was to be alert for whatever came in tomorrow. He ran through in his head the next day's work programme. Keep Sergeant Chambers on the mobile phone data and the two kids on Twitter. He'd continue too with officers door-knocking on every house in Wasdale. Not much of any interest had come through from their efforts so far, but somebody in the valley just might have heard something significant that night. You never knew. He'd have to put a search team back on the fells, too, for any more misplaced clothing or mobile phones. Then there were Meade's business affairs. He needed to know more about the caravan park or chalet park or whatever it was. He'd talk to his office manager, a very organised woman detective sergeant, about getting the financial information through. And of course he was already committed to taking that excursion to the morgue. Another busy day ahead.

Tuesday

1.

Tuesday dawned fair and Nick woke early. He put on running clothes and his well-used fell shoes and pulled the front door closed behind him, not bothering to lock it. His route took him eastwards from Grasmere across the main A591 and then on to the mountains, up to Great Rigg and then back down the ridge to Heron Pike before turning for home. Two thousand feet of climbing, give or take. It took him just under the hour door-to-door.

What a fantastic way to start a working day he thought as, showered, dressed and in his kitchen, he made coffee and put on the toast. What a contrast with his previous urban existence in London. His and Ana's house in Kentish Town had looked out on the bare brick wall of a neighbouring house whereas here he could see the fells in almost all directions from his cottage. And with those views had come a new passion for running, and especially fellrunning. What better way to explore his Lakeland neighbourhood than to run lightly and quickly over the mountain sides?

After the busyness of the day before Nick was looking forward to having time in his office. The remaining research for his Observer piece shouldn't take too long, and he might even be able to start the writing up later in the day. It would be good to be ahead of schedule for although Molly hadn't yet confirmed it he was expecting her to want him at the *Enquirer* all day Wednesday.

But the main task for the day was to finish off one of the two remaining chapters of *Nuclear Power – Yes Please?* He had lived with this book for much longer than he'd originally anticipated and his publishers had been remarkably tolerant when he failed to deliver by the original deadline, but he knew that the book as it had already developed was one of the best things he'd ever done. Another few weeks would be enough, and the manuscript would be on its way to London.

Not that the book had been easy to write. The plan had been to explain how it was that an industry which had seemed heading for extinction following the Chernobyl melt-down in 1986 had managed to bounce back at the start of the twenty-first century. Even the terrible events at Fukushima in 2011 hadn't stopped the forward march of new nuclear power plants, both in Britain and abroad. Why were politicians suddenly prepared to contemplate nuclear power again – and who was making the money?

His research had involved him talking both to opponents of nuclear power, including a helpful contact he had got to know at Greenpeace, and to the slick and efficient pro-nuclear business lobby. Of course, there were arguments advanced on both sides of what had become a very acrimonious dispute. There were a number of once-prominent anti-nuclear activists who had changed their minds, generally on the basis that nuclear power provided a better alternative than reliance on fossil fuels and greenhouse gas emitting energy generation. But there were also the steadfast campaigners who, more than thirty years after they had first pinned on a 'Nuclear Power? No thanks!' badge, were still raising the issue. Nuclear power, they claimed, was inherently dangerous and colossally expensive.

Nick's book covered the argument, but his real focus was on the business side of the industry. An old friend who was now features editor at New Scientist had given him some helpful early leads and he'd also picked the brains of a number of university academics who covered the field. He had researched in detail the French state-owned energy giant EDF, one of the protagonists in the plans for Hinkley Point in Somerset. He had a section written on another major French firm, the reactor manufacturer Areva. He was probably by now one of the best-informed people outside Japan on the business affairs of Tepco, Tokyo Electric Power, the company which owned the Fukushima power station. He even had a research folder on his desk for the Finnish nuclear firm Teollisuuden Voima and its much delayed efforts to open a new nuclear plant on Finland's Gulf of Bothnia coast.

The real challenge had been to lift the secrecy on China's nuclear industry, and in particular the two companies China General Nuclear and China National Nuclear Corporation, both now of considerable significance since they had been lined up in 2015 by the British government for the proposed Hinkley Point project. Nick had struggled initially to tackle this part of the story but had eventually, through a series of leads, been put in touch with a Chinese dissident who liked to call himself 'the Professor'. Whether he had genuine academic credentials or not, the Professor had certainly had access to some fascinating documents which he seemed happy to pass on.

Nick didn't entirely trust him and could never work out quite where the Professor's money came from, but he had carefully checked out the information he had been given and had every reason to believe it was genuine. Genuine, and fascinating.

His first telephone call of the day once he was upstairs in the spare bedroom which doubled as his office was to the Professor. The ringing tone on the man's mobile suggested the call was being transferred abroad and eventually the voicemail cut in. Nick pondered ringing off but in the end left a message: "Professor, Nick Potterton here. A very small query. You mentioned the popular protests at the Pengze reactor site on the Yangtze river to me once before. I need to check that these were in 2011? Anything going on there now? I'm on my usual number."

He rang off and then telephoned the main press office in Greenpeace's International office in Amsterdam, this time to clarify the position in South Korea where the state had approved the building of the world's largest nuclear plant. The third call went through to his editor at his publishing company, to brief her on the progress he was making. In the past these calls had sometimes been difficult, but now most of the book was safely on his computer and on a back-up memory stick. Give me another four weeks, he'd told her, and the full text will be with you. She'd said reassuringly positive things back to him and had told him that the marketing department would be in touch shortly.

Nick had hardly come off the phone before it rang.

"Morning, Nick." It was Molly Everett.

"Morning, Molly," he replied.

Molly might have started her career at the *Cumbrian Enquirer* as a junior reporter but her promotion to the editor's chair had seemed an inevitable progression. Nick rated her highly as a journalist. She could have had her pick of any number of jobs on the London dailies had she wanted them, but she chose instead to remain in Cumbria. Just a few years older than Nick, she had phenomenal local contacts in the most unlikely places and she knew instinctively what made a story.

She was a good colleague. But she'd not been easy to work with recently. Apart from journalism her other passion had always been for cigarettes and – despite what the law had to say about smoking

46

in the workplace – the office of the *Enquirer* had always reeked of stale tobacco. No longer: Molly had had a health scare a year or so back and had been told categorically by her doctor that she had to give up on the cigarettes. It made for a much better air quality at work, but it also had made Molly snappy and short-tempered. Now she was vaping away at her e-cigarette almost constantly, although without any obvious pleasure.

"Know much about Richard Meade?" Molly had asked.

"The body up by Wasdale? It indirectly has got me a commission for the Observer." Nick briefly explained his Three Peaks story.

"George Mulholland isn't telling me what's going on. I suspect foul play."

"I got turned back yesterday when I tried to go up to the site. Young police constable there told me it was a crime scene."

"Crime scene? That's interesting," Molly replied.

"Yes, I've been trying not to get side-tracked from my Observer piece into finding out more about Meade." One of the first rules of journalism was to stick to the job in hand, write the article and then move on. "Although I've been tempted," he added.

Nick briefly told Molly of his trip down to Greensleeves. "A disaffected handyman and some unhappy elderly residents, possibly with dementia. Nothing unusual there. Meade himself seems to have been a pillar of the local Rotary Club. Mind you, the Three Peaks guide I tried to interview seemed very rattled about something. Guy called Rug, lives Kendal."

"Not young Rugglesdon?"

"You know him?" Molly's contacts were really extraordinary, Nick thought.

"He has a bit of a reputation. Tries his hand at all sorts of things but never seems to settle down. His mother's Amanda Rugglesdon and, poor woman, she doesn't know what to do with him. Amanda runs the local Arts Festival. Surprised you don't know her. I maybe might give her a ring."

By which Nick understood that Molly would be on the phone to her immediately their own call was terminated.

"Want me tomorrow, Molly?" he asked. Not long ago he'd been regularly working three days at the *Enquirer*. More recently, it had gone down to two days and this week for the first time it might be a single day, or so it seemed. Nick had other work to do but enjoyed being back in the atmosphere of a busy newsroom, even if it was only for a weekly local paper.

There was a slight pause. "Perhaps just tomorrow afternoon, for any final subbing. Tell you what, I'll take you to lunch first."

Half a day: that was a surprise. So indeed was the offer of lunch on the day the paper went to press. "Financial position still worrying?" Nick asked.

"Not great," Molly replied. "I'll tell you tomorrow. Bye for now."

She rang off and Nick plunged back into the world of Chinese nuclear power. But he'd hardly had the chance to type more than a few lines when the desk phone rang again. He sighed, picked it up and gave his name.

"It's Monica here." It was a woman's voice, sounding timid.

"Monica?" Who did Nick know on first name terms called Monica?

"You gave me your card yesterday. When you came to Greensleeves. And you told me all about being in mountain rescue."

Realisation dawned. "I did. Tell me, Monica, are the blisters better?"

"Still very raw," she answered. There was a pause.

"I'm worried and I didn't know who else to ring. You seemed very friendly yesterday," she went on.

Well, yes, I'm a journalist, Nick thought to himself. There were several skills which helped if you wanted to do your job properly in the journalism business. You had to be able to write, of course, to know the law and ideally to have some shorthand, but you also had to know how to ask the questions which got the answers you needed. Nick liked to think that he was honest and above-board in the way he approached his trade, but he did know that somehow he had acquired a knack of gaining people's confidence. It had stood in him good stead many times in the past.

"Why are you worried?" he replied.

"Mr Meade's not come back and" – a pause – "and everyone thinks he's dead." And then in a rush: "If he's dead, I don't know who's going to pay me and I don't even know if I should be working because I'm on a zero hours contract and it was Mr Meade who told me if he needed me or not at the start of each week and I'm in the office now but perhaps I shouldn't be and perhaps I haven't got a job any more." There was the sound of a stifled sob.

Damn, Nick thought, Richard Meade is the story which won't go away. And I'm not even being paid to write it up.

Nick made a sympathetic noise. "Isn't there anyone in charge you could ask?"

"Peggy's trying to keep the office going, but it's terrible. And the police were waiting to talk to us again when we got in at nine. More questions about the weekend. And about what Mr Meade was like."

"Monica, I do understand how distressing this is. You all need someone to offer you support." A thought came to Nick. "Do you know who the new owner of Greensleeves would be if Mr Meade is indeed not going to be coming back?"

"No!" Monica almost screamed her reply. "Nobody knows who owns Greensleeves any more. Can you help us find out?"

"Well…" Nick was momentarily nonplussed. He looked at the display on his phone which told him the number calling him. "Well, I'd have to see. Is this your mobile number you're on now? I'll ring you back if I manage to get any more information. Look after yourself."

"I'll try to." Another sniff from the other end of the line. "Thank you, I knew you'd be able to help me." And the call ended.

2.

So, she asked herself as she sipped the froth from her cappuccino, how was she feeling about all this?

She was feeling, she realised, a lot more distraught than she had expected. It wasn't the fact that she had just come from looking at a corpse. She was a nurse, she had seen dead people before this.

No, it was the fact that this was not how she had expected it would finish, the story of the part of her life when she was married to, and then divorced from, Richard Meade. You stupid man, she had felt like crying out when she had been there in the morgue, you stupid man, what have you done now, why have you died?

Formal identification had been straightforward. It had been a long journey in the car from Barton-upon-Humber and she had started around five o'clock, stopping once on the M62 for a fry-up and coffee and then again in Keswick where she had picked up Adam, who had taken over the driving from her. Her younger son Dan had offered to come with her as well but he had college courses in Hull all day and she was keen to ensure that he got decent A level grades next summer.

And so Adam had had the task of driving the car along the slow A66 from Keswick to west Cumbria. At the police station they'd met a young woman detective constable who introduced herself as Susie and a much older detective whose name she missed but who was obviously in charge. The four of them had made the necessary visit. The body was most definitely Richard's, although at the same time it wasn't. His personality, his stubborn stroppy self that she had first loved and then hated, had fled from the body.

Adam had been in a difficult mood throughout the whole morning, not himself at all. It was as if he was locked away inside himself, beyond her reach. She would have appreciated more support from her son, but perhaps she was being unreasonable. Perhaps he needed supporting more than she did. He was 21, obliged to act the man but far too young really to have to live through an experience like this.

He'd taken the wheel again, when the business had been dealt with and they were heading back in the opposite direction on the A66, but only as far as Keswick. He was in a hurry to get back to work in time for the lunchtime rush, he'd told her. Well, she could understand that. This was, after all, his first real job. He'd got his catering qualification at Hull College twelve months back and had got a summer post working in the kitchen of a tourist pub in Keswick earlier in the year. It was, he'd told her, a pub with pretensions when it came to the bar food on offer. He'd taken the accommodation the pub provided and moved out from the small bedroom he'd occupied in her home since she'd moved to Humberside after the divorce. One bird flown, one still in the nest.

So after saying goodbye to Adam in Keswick she was left alone in the car, facing the long haul back to Barton. She pulled over just before the motorway at a roadside café and ordered a coffee and sandwich. And then she felt a desolation she had not experienced before.

She was Paula Pettifer now again, having reverted to her maiden name after the divorce, but she had been Paula Meade for fifteen years and Adam and Dan were the fruits of that relationship. And of course she had loved Richard. Well, certainly initially. His determination, his energy, his power to make what he wanted happen, all this was what had made him special for her. They'd met shortly after she had turned twenty-four and he was twenty-five. They'd both had relationships before but this felt like the special one which would last a lifetime. She had worn an off-the-shoulder white bridal dress with exquisite lace trimming. Richard had told her she had looked stunning. She knew she had.

And he was stunning that day, too, in a morning suit he'd had made for him specially. This is too big a day for me to wear hired clothes, he'd said. There was no doubt that he carried a sharply tailored suit very well. He took pride in his appearance. He wanted to ensure he got the respect that he knew he deserved.

So why had it all unravelled? It had unravelled so slowly that she'd hardly been aware of what was happening until they'd reached the point of no return. She had moved out, with Adam and Dan. She had instructed solicitors. He had instructed solicitors. God, it had been painful.

The image of the body in the morgue returned to her unprompted. So why hadn't things worked out? It was the sense that, as the years had passed, Richard had become more and more secretive. What she had found hard to take was the sense that he was deliberately keeping her in the dark about things. She no longer knew what he was up to, or what was happening with his business. In fact, she felt she no longer knew him.

She had grown little by little to dislike the very things that she had once found so attractive in Richard Meade. His single-minded determination had migrated into something else, an obsession with getting his own way. His power to make things happen could seem like arrogance.

He'd used his power over Adam and Dan too, poor lads. The grief he'd given Adam, for example, that time when he'd learned that Adam had set his heart on a career in catering rather than doing the business management degree Richard had told him to go for. Just recently she'd thought that the father and son relationship might be a little on the mend. Adam had seen more of his father recently than she had. Perhaps that was why Adam seemed so knocked back at the reality of Richard's death.

She absent-mindedly put the sandwich in her mouth, discovering with some surprise that it tasted of curried chicken. Somehow she had thought she was buying egg mayonnaise. She needed to pull herself together for the return journey.

Back to her small rented house. It had been a wrench to leave the comfort of what the boys had always called Fawlty Towers but she was pleased to have space of her own again. A chance to make a new life for herself. Had Richard dunned her in the divorce settlement? Probably, she suspected that his solicitor was sharper than hers and anyway Richard always had accountants' reports to hand to demonstrate that Greensleeves was worth almost nothing. At least they'd agreed that Adam and Dan would have half the shares in the business between them as part of the settlement. She wondered vaguely what would happen now Richard was dead. More expensive solicitors' fees, she imagined.

She took another bite of the chicken sandwich and then, to her complete embarrassment, burst into loud sobs. She was aware of the other café customers looking at her askance. One couple left immediately.

The woman on the check-out came towards her. She had become, she realised, a Problem. She muttered something to the woman about a family bereavement, and left for her car immediately. Half a cup of cappuccino and half a sandwich remained behind, unfinished.

Wednesday

1.

Sergeant Chrissy Chambers checked that her uniform was in order before knocking on the office door. DCI Mulholland had asked to see her.

It was not something she would admit – certainly not if the police investigation into this man Richard Meade did turn out to be a murder enquiry – but she had very much enjoyed the last few days. She had joined the Cumbrian police after doing a sociology degree at Newcastle and getting a good 2.1, one of the increasing number of talented graduates who were turning to the police for a career. The old days when you joined the police after school at 15 or 16 as a cadet and slowly made your way up the ladder had changed. The promotion to sergeant had come quickly, before she had turned thirty, and she was ready now for further challenges. But her attempt to transfer to the CID a year back had been knocked back. Not enough experience, they'd told her.

There was a lot she found really attractive about her chosen job, but sometimes the tradition of the police force drove her crazy. That, and the obsessive importance the police gave to rank and hierarchy. Friends from Uni now working in the private sector told her that these days good businesses emphasised networking and partnership and collaborative working and all that sort of stuff. Nobody had yet appeared to convey that message to the police.

So the opportunity which, by sheer luck, had come her way to work with DCI Mulholland on this case was one she intended to use to the full. She had only known Mulholland by repute before, as something of a throw-back to old-style policing. He seemed to relish his reputation in this respect. He had even come to work on Monday morning sporting a cravat.

His curiously antique way of saying things remained, too, but Chambers had now had the chance to watch him at close quarters and she liked what she saw. He'd got the enquiry up and running from a standing start and had drawn together a team of junior officers whom she assessed as having real talent. So it certainly wasn't Mulholland's fault that the investigation was still waiting for the break-through.

"Sergeant Chambers," Mulholland had said as she entered the room. "Welcome once again to my little corner of hell." (It was true, Chambers thought, the office was not as salubrious as it had been on Monday morning, a vaguely disquieting odour hanging on the air.) "The tenth circle of hell."

"Excuse me, sir, doesn't hell stop at just nine circles?"

"Quite right to correct me, Sergeant. My remembrance of Dante is slipping. Good to know your brain is working well today." He gestured to her to sit down and posed an opening question.

"Meade's mobile phone. Tell me what we know."

"We're not as far ahead as we'd like. We know pretty well who he had been ringing in the days leading up to his death, but nothing really stands out. Lots of calls to his Greensleeves site office, calls to various other business people, a local restaurant, the golf club, the newsdesk at the Blackpool Gazette which was probably about his charity fundraising, some calls we've traced to a financial adviser, some calls to his solicitor too. We're liaising with Lancashire to check all these contacts out further. The data's all here."

"Good. Any calls to women?"

"Almost none, or at least none to phone numbers registered to women users. If there was a girlfriend on the scene, he either didn't talk to her much or used a different phone. But there is one quite important thing. In the forty-eight hours before his death he made five calls to the same mobile number."

"...Belonging to?" Mulholland prompted her.

"This is the problem. The number is allocated to a pay-as-you-go phone which was bought at the O2 store in Blackpool a year ago. The phone was bought by Richard Meade himself."

"He was obviously not phoning himself."

"No, sir, we assume he had given the phone to someone else to use. But the records show that the phone was never used to make any outward calls, so we've got little to go on. The network's checking to see if we can find out where the incoming calls were received. The phone's GPS function was turned off, by the way."

"Pity. What about his twittering?"

"Tweeting, yes. Again nothing that stands out. He had about a hundred followers, many of them trade and business."

"All right. I want you to interview the Three Peaks guide again, Mr Rugglesdon. I've been looking at the notes of the first interview with him and to be honest your uniformed colleagues didn't push him hard enough first time round. Choose someone you trust to accompany you. I suggest you ask Rugglesdon to attend the Kendal station. It's always better when we're on home territory and they're playing away. Makes them sweat a little."

There was a knock and the enquiry's office manager, an older woman detective sergeant who had been given by Mulholland the task of pulling together all the material coming back from the leads being followed, put her head round the door. Chrissy Chambers made to leave, but Mulholland waved her back into her seat. "No need to go," he said.

"Toxicology finally back, and it's negative for drugs," the DS told Mulholland, passing across a sheaf of papers.

"Hmm, doesn't mean he wasn't drugged of course," Mulholland responded.

"No, sir. And you need to read the forensics report which is also here. Nothing very interesting about the trousers, unfortunately. The waterproof jacket is also linked to Meade. Sweat, I gather." More papers were passed to Mulholland.

"The shirt?"

"Nothing back yet. I'm chasing. Forensics know it's urgent."

Chrissy Chambers must have shown surprise, for Mulholland turned towards her. "Yes, two PCs found Meade's shirt yesterday. Or at least, somebody's shirt. Neatly folded up as if coming back from the laundry and placed in a small gap at the bottom of a rock, about half a mile from the body. Don't know how it got missed first time round."

Mulholland turned back to address his office manager. "Kate, we'll call a press conference tomorrow morning. Not sure yet how we'll play it, but the *Enquirer* will be out by then and we may need to respond. Their esteemed editor Molly Everett is being exceptionally coy with me about what she knows. Get the conference set up with the media team, will you?"

He turned back to the papers on his desk. It was a cue. Chrissy Chambers responded and quietly left the room.

2.

Life had suddenly caught up with Adam Meade and punched him hard in the solar plexus.

After saying goodbye to his mother at Tuesday lunchtime he had wandered back to work barely able to speak, let alone organise the right quantity of coulis for the duck breasts or whatever it was he was supposed to be preparing. Chef had shouted at him twice, telling him to wake up, telling him to stop being a twat. As Adam had not wanted to tell Chef or anyone at work where he had been that morning, he felt he couldn't complain.

By the evening it was obvious to everyone that he was not well. They'd let him go at six o'clock. He had gone straight to his tiny room in the pub annexe without eating. Sleep did not come however. At around eight he was violently sick into the toilet bowl and at ten or so he was sick again. Delayed reaction to the visit to the morgue he told himself. Eventually he must have slept, because he woke on Wednesday morning at the usual time. Outside the roof-light window there was the sound of a town shaking itself awake. Life was going on just as normal, apparently.

It had been a shock, that visit. And the two police officers, especially the older detective, who had seemed to be there just to eye him up to see what crimes they could pin on him. He was a twenty-one year old man and everyone knew that young men committed all the crimes going, so obviously he must be guilty of something.

His Dad was dead. Seeing the body there had made it an incontestable reality. The last time he'd met his father they'd parted on bad terms. He thought of what he would have wanted to say to make amends. He would have wanted to say that, despite everything that had come between them, he loved his father. But it was too late now for anything like this. Corpses can't make conversation.

He had been both happy and lonely in Keswick. He had been happy to have for the first time his own place, basic though it was. His mother had been good to him and Dan but he couldn't stay in her house for ever and anyway he'd never taken to their new life in Humberside. He had been happy too to have met Chelsii. They'd had some good times together on his nights off and some very good times later on in his tiny single bed. She had a great body. But Chelsii had gone out of his life several weeks ago. It hadn't worked out. He had to admit that his father had helped break up the relationship, having been critical of Chelsii right from the start. "Get yourself a woman with some get up and go," he'd told her. "Chelsii's too laid back. Spells her name in a strange way, too. Not your type, son."

So now he was finding Keswick a lonely town, full of tourists trying to escape the Lake District rain and poorly-paid locals trying to make the most of the tourists before the autumn and the winter came and work started drying up. His own contract was only until early October, and he had no idea what he would do after that.

But in the meantime the tourists wanted their meals, and these days they wanted something more than bangers and mash and baked beans. What they seemed to want more than anything was organic Cumberland sausage with buttery celeriac puree served with a light onion gravy made with beer from the local microbrewery, and with a nice dessert to follow. Almost always crème brulée.

He made his way down to the kitchen for the breakfast shift, which he was required to do four days a week. Several orders came in for the scrambled eggs and smoked salmon, and he enjoyed the distraction of breaking the eggs and watching them turn into a light yellow emulsion as they cooked. At 9.30 the shift ended and he had free time until lunch.

But just before then Life came to get him once again. The owner of the pub sought him out, carrying a large brown envelope. "Special delivery, Adam. Must be love letters!"

It was a letter from a firm of solicitors he had never heard of, based in Manchester. He couldn't understand what they were saying but he could understand very well that the letter was serious. It appeared to suggest that he was now deemed to have responsibility for what they called The Green Sleeves Residential Park, and that as such he was advised of the debt which was due to their client and required payment blah blah. We look forward to your earliest communication blah blah.

He had given very little thought to the implications of his father's death for Greensleeves. He had never understood quite what the deal had been after the divorce but he knew that some sort of trust had been created by his father with half of Greensleeves' shares. Dan and he were to be the beneficiaries once they turned eighteen. Dan wasn't there yet of course but Adam had for the past three years received on an irregular basis from his father various envelopes of papers, with instructions on where his signature was needed. And then, in between these papers, some less frequent envelopes which came with cheques drawn to him on Greensleeves' business account. The cheques always seemed to be for quite small amounts but anything was welcome.

He should, he knew, have given more attention to the paperwork, but his father had told him not to worry and that these were just formalities. His father could be persuasive, if not positively demanding, when he wanted to be.

Now his father had bequeathed him what appeared to be a mega-problem. He needed someone to talk to. He went out into Main Street where most of Keswick's shops congregated and entered the first solicitors' firm he could find. A young receptionist, quite a good-looking woman with blonde wavy hair and nice teeth, was at the front desk. The first possible appointment with one of the firm's solicitors was at 9 o'clock on Friday, she told him, and the first session would be charged at a flat £45 plus VAT. Thereafter, if he wanted to instruct them, there would be an hourly charge. This would all be explained to him. Did he want the appointment? She gave him a big smile.

Adam had anticipated being able to see someone there and then, but clearly this was the way these things worked. Anyway, it would be good to have the opportunity to see the receptionist again. He accepted, giving his name and address.

He had just left the office and was moseying aimlessly in the vague direction of Keswick's moot hall when his mobile rang. The day was about to take a further unexpected turn.

It was a woman's voice he didn't recognise. "Hello, is that Adam?" it said. "You don't know me, but my name's Josie and I know your father. In fact, I know him well. Knew him well," she corrected herself. There was a moment of silence. "I'm his girlfriend. And I need to talk to you urgently. Can I meet you this afternoon? You're in Keswick, I know, I can drive there. Three o'clock. Suppose we meet outside the Alhambra cinema?"

Three o'clock – between the lunch and dinner shifts. Had his father told this woman about his job? He presumed he must have.

"OK, I guess so." Adam felt he had no alternative.

"Good, don't be worried," she'd said, and rung off.

3.

Nick worked until midday, satisfactorily polishing off his Observer article and emailing it through to Martin Eveyard. It was ready a day before Martin's deadline, exactly to length and (he said to himself) a pretty competent piece of journalism. Yes, he could still deliver the goods.

Molly had told him where she was suggesting they met for lunch, a rough and ready coffee place just round the corner from the *Enquirer's* office. It was not exactly the sort of chichi winebar where London-based journalists might be seen socialising with their commissioning editors but never mind, this was Cumbria. This was real life.

Molly was there already, sitting looking restless. Coming off nicotine addiction had been hard work, not just for her but for all her friends and colleagues too.

"Lunch with my editor. This is an unusual treat," Nick had begun.

"Don't count on it happening again. Anyway, I'm deducting what you eat from your wages this week."

"Thank you, Molly. I expected no less." Molly was known for her interesting dress sense and today was no exception. She had on a bright purple fisherman's smock which hung somewhat precipitously over her large bosom. Underneath could be seen an equally bright pink blouse.

"Paper looking OK?" Nick enquired.

"Nearly there. I'm running the Wasdale body on page one. I spoke to Rug by the way."

"Did he fess up?"

Molly laughed. "No, but he's a very worried young man at the moment. He had no public liability insurance and he suddenly thinks that it would have been a good idea. And he's worried that the police will find out he was the person driving the minibus all round Britain as well as guiding the walkers up and down the mountains."

"Sounds dodgy."

"I don't know the rules about minibus driving but it doesn't sound very sensible to me. Anyway, it's not really relevant to the story I'm running. Rug told me off the record and I'll respect that."

"Still think it was foul play?"

"Not sure, but probably. George is still being very elusive, by the way."

"You can never trust the police," Nick said.

"No, almost as bad as journalists." They both laughed.

"Got anything more you can offer me on Richard Meade?" Molly went on. "It was useful what you told me about the fellside being closed off by the police, incidentally."

"I've been trying to get on with paid work, but Mr Meade keeps getting in the way." Nick mentioned the phone call which had come through from one of the people he had interviewed at Greensleeves. "Out of interest I did a Companies House search and it was much less straightforward than I expected. The Greensleeves' shares are in the hands of a holding company, and that in turn has a parent company headquartered in the Isle of Man. Somebody has gone to a lot of trouble on this."

"Hmm. That's a different side to the Meade story from the one the Blackpool Gazette is covering." Molly passed across her tablet showing the lead story from the Gazette's website. Nick skim-read it.

"The businessman with a soft heart for local good causes."

"If I might put this crudely, the children's hospice can't believe its good fortune," Molly replied. "Richard Meade's JustGiving webpage has gone crazy since the news of his death. Already over £50,000 has been pledged, by complete strangers."

"The British people are basically good-hearted."

"Yes, they are. I'm afraid I'm using this angle too. We've got a picture of Meade at the hospice surrounded by smiling children."

"Of course." Molly knew this was the story her readers would want to read. Nick would have done the same in her place.

"What I did glean from the company returns is that Greensleeves was either making a hefty loss or was diverting its profits somewhere else. If Meade had money worries that might point to a suicide," Nick went on.

"Bit of a pantomime to organise the whole Three Peaks thing just to top yourself."

"Yes, that's true," Nick conceded. "Meade also showed up as a director of a firm called Rosy Retirement Planning Ltd, although the firm didn't seem to be trading. Or at least filing accounts."

"You're pretending you're back on the Sunday Times Insight team. Concentrate on the school plays and the dog shows, that's what people want to read."

"Thank you for the career advice, Molly. Actually, I may have to see if the Sunday Times has any work for me. Given that the *Cumbrian Enquirer* doesn't seem to love me any more or want my work."

Molly sighed. "That's what I wanted to talk to you about. Over lunch, rather than just in the office. I'm not sure how much longer I'll have any work either."

She shared with Nick in broad terms what the *Enquirer's* accountant had said on Monday.

"Don't suppose you've got any money you'd like to invest? And probably lose?" It was a half-serious question from Molly.

"Well, a little but not much and I'd rather not lose it. Do you think the Greet family members want to sell?"

"John and Teresa? Probably, although they'll expect more for the paper than they should. People always expect long-established businesses to be worth a lot. They don't realise they've had the profits out as dividends year after year."

"Could we arrange a management buy-out? An employee buy-out?" Nick suddenly had an idea. "Crowdfunding. Get the readers to put in some capital too. I did a piece a few years back on a local newspaper on the French Riviera that did just this and got hundreds of thousands of euros in from readers. Worth a thought. *Enquirer* readers are very loyal."

"It's possible, perhaps. Maybe we can talk this through in more detail later in the month. I'm arranging to see a business adviser next week. John Wythenshawe is a lovely man but his duty is primarily to work for John and Teresa's interest over this. Anyway, we need to get back to work."

So much, Nick thought, for the old tradition of long boozy lunch-hours which Fleet Street had once been famous for. Lunch had been a bowl of carrot and sweet potato soup, lightly curried and served with a stale brown roll. Nick finished his bowl and pushed back his chair. Molly went across to the counter and paid.

4.

The young man with the beard who had opened the front door in Kendal to Sergeant Chambers looked as if he was shitting himself. Good, she thought.

"Thank you for agreeing to accompany us to the station," she had said, showing him to the back seat of the police car. "This is my colleague, PC Whittaker." The woman in the driver's seat turned to acknowledge him.

Chrissy Chambers had booked one of the interview rooms at Kendal police station. It had taken her and Rosie Whittaker the best part of two hours to drive across from Whitehaven and she intended to make sure the journey was worthwhile.

She'd sat him down on the metal chair in front of the desk and taken her own seat behind it. PC Whittaker had offered him a glass of water, which he had declined.

Rosie Whittaker had then set the digital recorder working, before taking her own seat alongside Chrissy Chambers.

Chambers formally cautioned him, a necessary step if the interview was later to be usable as evidence. He wasn't under arrest, she explained. He could leave at any time.

"You're not arresting me?" Rugglesdon had queried back at her.

"No, Mr Rugglesdon," Chambers had replied. She had resisted the temptation to add: "Why, should I be?"

She and Whittaker had discussed the shape of the interview in the car coming over. She didn't know how long Rugglesdon thought he would be at the police station but she expected the session to be a long one. Two hours min, she thought.

She began gently. Full name, permanent address, date of birth, occupation.

Rugglesdon blanched even at these questions. God, he was a nervy customer she thought. He paused at the question on his occupation and eventually responded in a quiet voice, "Mountain guide."

She smiled encouragingly at him. "Good. Now I want to discuss what happened last weekend step by step. Let's start at the very beginning, shall we?"

The first questions were designed to reassure and they seemed to be having the desired effect. Chambers had arranged to ask him to describe in quite unnecessary detail the journey north on Saturday morning. Rugglesdon gradually relaxed.

"So you stopped the minibus at one of the service stations going north on the A74(M). Can you remember which one?" Rugglesdon had gone into a long ramble about motorway service areas.

The questioning finally reached Wasdale and the early hours of Sunday morning. Chambers abruptly changed her approach.

"Why didn't Mr Meade accompany you up Scafell Pike?" she asked aggressively.

Rugglesdon looked uncomfortable. "He was on his phone. He told us he'd catch us up."

"But it was bad weather and the middle of the night. Why didn't you wait for him?"

"I suppose – I suppose I should have done. But Mr Meade was insistent. He said he knew the way."

"But he didn't catch you up?"

"No. So eventually I told the others we'd have to go back. They weren't happy."

"And?"

"And Mr Meade wasn't at the minibus. You know this already."

"Tell me anyway."

"So eventually I went to the hotel and knocked somebody up and got them to ring the police."

"Could you get into the minibus?"

"No. It was locked."

"Why?"

"I don't know."

"Really?"

There was a pause. "I'd left the key on the driver's seat. I thought Mr Meade would see it and bring it." Another pause. "The rental company told me when I picked up the minibus that it had a self-locking security feature. They told me not to lose the key. Other people had locked themselves out, apparently."

"So...."

"I guess Mr Meade must have pulled the passenger door closed behind him and the minibus lock came on. I've felt awful about this ever since. But it was Mr Meade's fault too."

Rug Rugglesdon looked on the brink of collapsing into tears. Chambers moved to a new subject.

"What was Mr Meade saying on the phone?"

"I don't know."

"He was on his mobile phone a great deal that evening. He was sitting next to you. You must have heard what he said."

Rugglesdon looked even more desperate. "I deliberately didn't listen. It was his private business. Anyway I had to concentrate on the driving."

"How did he sound? Pleased? Angry? Worried?"

"It was hard to say really."

"When you'd parked at Wasdale Head and you no longer had to concentrate on the road, Mr Meade was still on the phone, wasn't he."

"Yes." This came out accompanied by almost a sob.

"So what was he saying then?"

"I don't know, I couldn't tell."

"All right Mr Rugglesdon. How well did you know Mr Meade?"

"He rang me up about a month ago. He wanted a guide for his Three Peaks challenge."

"And you agreed?" A nod and a stifled 'yes' in reply.

"How much did you charge Mr Meade?"

"I... I agreed I'd do it for a hundred pounds."

"A hundred pounds! You're a professional mountain guide and you charged him a hundred pounds for a whole weekend's work?"

"He beat me down. I wanted £750. He told me I was taking money from the children in the hospice. He was very insistent." A pause. "He said he'd pay for the minibus."

"How much have you charged previous Three Peaks groups you've led?"

A reply, in a small voice: "I've not done it before."

"I see. How did Mr Meade know about your services?"

Rugglesdon looked even unhappier. "My mother... You see, my mother was sitting next to him at a North-West charity fundraiser dinner in Lancaster earlier this year. I think my mother told him I could organise the Three Peaks for him. She gave him my contact details. He rang a few days later."

"You had never met him before?"

"No." This said with more confidence.

"You didn't know him socially? Or professionally?"

"No."

"And after Wasdale Head, tell me what would have happened next if Mr Meade had not gone missing and the minibus had not unhelpfully locked itself."

"Snowdon. We were going to do Snowdon."

"Let me get this absolutely straight, Mr Rugglesdon. You drove the hired minibus, as you have told us, from where you had parked it outside your house in Kendal at 4am on Saturday morning south to pick up Mr Meade and his colleagues at 5am at the Greensleeves park entrance. And then you drove up the motorway to Glasgow and from there north to Fort William. Then you escorted the group of walkers up Ben Nevis and down again. And then you drove them in the minibus south to Glasgow and then on the motorway to Penrith where you left the M6 to drive to Wasdale Head. There you intended to guide your party to the top of Scafell Pike and down again. And then you intended to drive to north Wales and guide your party up and down Snowdon. And then you intended to drive the minibus back to Lancashire and eventually Kendal. Am I right?"

Silence.

"Am I right?" insistently.

"Yes."

"Where were you going to sleep on Saturday night?"

Pause. "I wasn't."

"Did you have any other drivers with you?"

Pause. "No."

"Did you have any other mountain guides with you?"

Pause. "No."

"All right, Mr Rugglesdon, we'll leave it there for today. PC Whittaker will arrange for you to get home."

The interview had lasted almost two and a half hours. Chambers formally declared the interview over, giving the closing time for the benefit of the recording. PC Whittaker switched off the machine. Rugglesdon rose to his feet and shambled from the room.

5.

Adam Meade had arrived outside Keswick's little independent cinema just before three. It was now ten past, and Josie the purported girlfriend showed no sign of materialising.

He looked up and down the road. He would wait another five minutes and then go back to the pub. He was needed in the kitchen by four and he had to change back into his whites beforehand.

He thought of the evening's shift and wondered if this time he would be able to get through it all right. He knew there was a large party of twenty or so already booked in. It was going to be busy.

"You must be Adam." A strange man had approached him, and was holding out his hand. "Sorry, I know you're waiting for someone else but I can explain. I'm Geoff."

The man was probably in his early forties, with a mop of fair hair. He was smartly dressed in a well-cut three-piece suit made of contemporary tweed and had some expensive looking brogues on his feet. He had his shirt unbuttoned at the collar.

Adam had made no reply so the man continued. "Actually, it's me that you're expecting. I'm really sorry I'm late. The motorway was fine but the road in from Penrith was terribly slow."

"I'm sorry, I don't understand. I had a call this morning from a woman who said she was my father's girlfriend."

"Yes – " The man paused. "Josie is a friend of mine and I asked her if she minded ringing you. She's an actor. I wanted to meet you and I wasn't sure how else to make the first approach. Josie isn't your dad's girlfriend. It's the other way round. I'm... Well I suppose you could say that I'm your dad's boyfriend."

Adam looked at the stranger, wondering if he could believe anything being said to him.

"I don't know who you are but I do know that my dad wasn't gay. He was married to my mother for over fifteen years."

"Yes, I know all about it. Richard has told me. You and Dan and your mother living in a small town somewhere near Hull. I think he genuinely loved your mother. Even if he was unfaithful. He told me he had flings with a whole host of people he met along the way. He was bi. He was special and I loved him, even if he did like to get his own way."

Adam had anticipated that the rendezvous with Josie might be best undertaken over a cup of coffee and maybe a cake at a local café. But faced with the very solid presence of Geoff in front of him, he changed his mind.

"I'm sorry, Mr…"

"Handley, but call me Geoff"

"I'm sorry, but I don't want to know any of this and I don't want to talk. I want you to go away right now."

"I will. I'm sorry, Adam, I suppose I didn't think through how this meeting would seem to you. But I just want you to know that I'm devastated too. I only heard indirectly through the media about Richard. I couldn't believe it. Friday he was full of life, boasting of how much sponsorship he'd got for the hospice. Please understand, I'm just desperate about it all and I can't mention it to anyone. People never really understand that a gay partner suffers bereavement in just the same way. I mean heterosexual people never understand, of course. And my relationship with Richard wasn't public knowledge. I've had no-one to talk to these last few days."

Geoff seemed as if he might break down at any moment. Adam reluctantly changed his mind. "There's a café near here where we can talk," he said. "But I have to warn you I need to be back at my work ready changed for four. I've only twenty minutes or so."

6.

Nick had settled down at his usual PC in the *Enquirer*'s office and logged on to the network. Molly had been right: this week's edition had already come together pretty well. He got to work subbing some of the inside news pages, correcting the odd rogue 'it's' when a simple third-person possessive 'its' was meant and devising appropriate headlines which fitted the space available. After an hour or so Molly put her head round his partition. She was vaping away for all she was worth. There was an unpleasant smell of something like eucalyptus.

"Front page done and dusted. Want to see?" she said.

Nick called up the page on his screen and together they inspected Molly's handiwork. She had chosen the main headline in a slightly larger point size than the *Enquirer* usually used. It read:

THE BODY IN THE BOG

– WAS IT MURDER?

There was a panel alongside which said '*Enquirer Exclusive*'. And indeed it was true. The *Enquirer* had something of a scoop on its hands here.

"You didn't need to have credited me, you know," Nick said. The article was by-lined with Molly Everett's name, with a line below which read 'Additional reporting by Nick Potterton'.

"Fair's fair. You gave me some helpful background. And I know how you like to keep cuttings with your by-line in a big scrapbook at home." They both laughed.

"Listen." More puffs on the e-cigarette before Molly continued: "I know this is unreasonably short notice, but could you manage another shift tomorrow? To start pulling things together for next week. George Mulholland has finally decided to have a press conference, at ten o'clock in Whitehaven of all places. I need to go, but I won't be back here until well after lunch, even if George spares us the homilies and the bons mots he loves so much."

"Yes, I think that should be OK. I finished the Observer piece this morning so there's nothing really pressing. All right if I come in about 9.30?"

"Fine." Their conversation was interrupted by Nick's mobile phone ringing in his pocket.

"What a nasty ring-tone," Molly said, waving him a farewell as she headed back to her office. Nick shrugged, and answered it.

"It's me," said the caller. "I have to talk to you, Nick. Can you come?"

"I'm sorry, who am I speaking to?"

"It's Monica. At the residential park. It's all gone awful today. Several of the residents have got all unpleasant. They say the toilet system has broken down and they need it fixed immediately. Peggy's tried to do something, but nobody's in charge and now the local council have got involved and there's somebody here walking around the site in a yellow jacket and he says he could close us down. And the residents say they are going to hold a demonstration at six. And we don't know who to talk to. And so I thought of you."

Nick sighed. His knowledge of sewage systems was zero and he also wasn't a therapist or counsellor. On the other hand he was a half-way decent journalist and this sounded too interesting to miss. Greensleeves was far outside the *Enquirer*'s circulation area so he couldn't cover this for the paper but on the other hand the *Enquirer* was almost ready to be put to bed for the week: Molly didn't need him in the office any longer.

"OK, Monica," he replied. "I will drive straight down. It will take me about an hour. Try to make sure nothing else happens until I'm there."

7.

"So what do we think?" The questioner was Sergeant Chrissy Chambers and she was in the police car talking to Rosie Whittaker. They had already been driving for well over an hour and were only somewhere near Broughton in Furness. Whitehaven was still an hour or so away.

"He was utterly petrified all the time. Are we really that scary?"

"I can be when I put my mind to it, so just watch your step PC Whittaker," Chrissy replied with a smile.

As the interminable Cumbrian miles had gone by outside the patrol car window Chambers had been reliving the interview with the young man Rugglesdon in her mind, point by point. She had learned during her time in the police how to structure interviews and how to extract the information she needed from witnesses and suspects, sometimes by guile and sometimes by playing on their fear, but she knew she still had more to learn. How had she done with Rugglesdon? If she was to get the transfer to the CID she was angling for, much would depend on how her superior officers judged her performance on occasions like these.

Generally, she thought the interview had gone well – not for Rugglesdon himself, of course, but that was how she had intended it. But had they really learned anything new? The business about the minibus locking system, perhaps. Did she believe that? Maybe. It sounded sufficiently unlikely to be the truth.

Rugglesdon had also mentioned that he'd called the police from the Wasdale Head hotel. Chrissy Chambers wasn't sure that this fact had emerged before. They'd have to send round uniformed officers to talk to the staff in the hotel, just to sign off that particular lead. Presumably the hotel was the nearest place to where the minibus had been parked. Careless of Rugglesdon not to have had an emergency mobile phone with him, but his whole approach had been shambolically amateur from beginning to end.

And then a sudden thought occurred to Chambers. "Listen," she said to Whittaker who was at the wheel of the patrol car, "if you turn off here we can take the minor road through Ulpha instead of the main road. It's nice countryside and not much further. And I have a sudden desire to see once again the beauty of Wasdale."

They turned, taking the lonely road across the fells to Eskdale Green before turning right to Nether Wasdale and Wasdale Head. At Chambers' instruction they parked near the National Trust campsite, a short distance before the hotel. This was where, less than a week before, Rugglesdon's party had set off for their abortive attempt on Scafell Pike.

"Get your phone out and ring the office, tell them we're running late," Chambers instructed Whittaker.

"The police radio?"

"No, your own mobile phone."

The police constable looked surprised but did as she was told. "Sorry, no signal," she said.

Chrissy Chambers pulled out her own personal mobile. "No signal on my phone either, not even 999 emergencies. Let's go and ask them in the hotel if they ever get mobile signals up here. But before we do let me bet you a pint that they'll laugh at us and say, 'Of course we don't, can't you see that there are mountains all around'."

There was a moment's pause, before Rosie Whittaker responded.

"But if there are no mobile signals, how did Meade get his phone to work?"

"That is what I would call a very good question, PC Whittaker."

8.

There was no demonstration. There was one hand-written placard, paper stuck roughly on cardboard, which read "Greensleeves residents say: don't treat us like s***", and an unhappy looking man behind it. There were four or five other older people grouped near him, whom Nick took to be fellow Greensleeves home owners. There was a solitary young PC watching them, looking self-important and eyeing up Nick with some hostility as he approached. And, clustered inside the office looking out, was a gaggle of staff, among whom Nick saw Monica, Peggy and Raisha. The handyman with the lump hammer seemed absent. So too was the yellow-jacketed council officer Monica had promised him. And so too, apart from Nick himself, was any sign of media interest.

Nick waved towards the office but approached the placard-man first. He had recognised him from his previous visit the day before and remembered his name.

"Hello again, Mr Trelawney," he said.

"Delighted to see you." The man was effusive. "Can we rely on the Observer to cover our plight?"

Nick offered a response which he hoped was both encouraging and noncommittal.

"Actually, we're just packing up here," the man went on. "Let me invite you back to my park home – it's the one over there with the roses outside. It'll be more comfortable than talking outside."

"Give me five minutes," Nick replied. "I just need to talk briefly with some of the staff." He made his way towards the office, greeting the young policeman as he passed with a 'Good evening officer' and getting a reluctant 'Good evening' back. The PC, he'd noticed, had written down his car number plate.

Monica unlocked the office door to let him in and gave him what, Nick felt, was a somewhat unnecessarily intimate hug. "We're so pleased to see you," she said, looking as if she might burst into tears. Nick gently extricated himself and was greeted next by Peggy, who offered her hand for him to shake. Several of the other staff he had met the day before were there too and in turn gave him handshakes.

"Thank you for coming again." Peggy was taking charge. "We could go through to the back office and talk there."

"Can I come back and see you all in half an hour or so? I have just committed to talking first to Mr Trelawney."

"Half an hour? You'll be lucky. He talks the hind-legs off a donkey, that man."

"All right, how late will you be here? What time are you going home?"

He saw Peggy and Monica exchange looks.

"Normally we'd be gone by now." Peggy was the speaker. "But I guess things aren't normal any more. A few of us were anyway talking about going up to the Traveller's Rest tonight, just to talk things over. That's the inn you passed as you drove in, up on the main road. I suppose we could meet you up there."

"Provided you promise us that you really will come." This was Monica.

Nick laughed. "I promise. I'll be as quick as I can with Mr Trelawney, but drink your drinks quite slowly just in case."

He headed back into the main part of the site. The placard had disappeared and the policeman was gone as well.

Awaiting him inside 'Rose Bower' was a reception party. Mr Trelawney got up to let him in, and made the introductions. "Jonathan

Forrest. Of course, you met him yesterday. This is Richard Delano. And this is my better half, Penelope." A woman came forward from the kitchen area and shook his hand.

"I invited Richard and Jonathan here, because we are the Greensleeves Residents' Association committee. Richard is our secretary and Jonathan is our treasurer. For my sins I am the Chairman."

"Residents' Association? I don't think I knew that you had an organisation like that," Nick replied.

"Ah, well, sore point. Mr Meade didn't recognise us, of course. Wouldn't give us the time of day. Living here was like being in a totalitarian state. Like East Germany. Before the wall came down, of course."

"But you had the association, nonetheless?" Nick was interested.

"We did, but we hadn't made the threshold so it was difficult." The speaker this time was Jonathan Forrest. He saw Nick looking puzzled, and went on. "Residential park owners only have to recognise a residents' association if 50% of the owners on the site are members. We never got that many, did we Peter?"

"We tried very hard, but no. People were frightened, you see." Peter Trelawney responded. "Of Mr Meade, I mean."

"I see," Nick said.

"He was a bastard, a right bastard." This was Richard Delano speaking now. "Shouldn't speak ill of the dead, but there's no point beating about the bush." Delano spoke with a strong Lancashire accent.

"You're right to be blunt, after how he treated you," said Forrest.

"He conned me good and proper," Delano replied.

"Gentlemen, Mr Potterton needs to hear what we have to say so he can tell his readers the truth. But the sun is firmly over the yard-arm. Before we start I propose beers all round."

As if on cue Penelope Trelawney approached with four glasses and four bottles of Sam Smith's.

"You're joining us, I hope?" Peter Trelawney said, looking at Nick.

"Go on, but just this one. My car's outside."

"Good man." Trelawney put a large ring-bound folder with Greensleeves R.A. written on it on the coffee table in front of Nick, opening it to reveal a stack of photocopied papers, all punch-holed.

At the top was a coloured booklet entitled *Park homes: know your rights.*

"It's all in here," Peter Trelawney said to Nick.

Nick laughed. "I'm sure it is, but why don't you tell me the problem you're facing in your own words? As succinctly as you can," he added hopefully.

Peter Trelawney needed no encouragement. "First you need to understand what the law says. It all changed a few years back. The Mobile Homes Act 2013, that's supposed to set out everything that happens here. Of course, it relies on residential park owners being law-abiding and playing by the book. Well, in our case..."

Nick interrupted. "You own your homes, don't you?" he asked. "So how does that work in relation to Mr Meade?"

"Ah, that's the nub of it," Trelawney replied. "We own our homes but we don't own the land. We have to pay a pitch fee for that. That goes to Meade."

"He can charge what he likes?"

"In the old days, yes. These days, he's supposed to justify any increase, and we can appeal to a tribunal. But I still think we pay far too much."

"And gas and electricity? And water?"

"Supplied by the park owner. Again, the charges used to be jacked up, allowing Meade to make a giant profit. Now it's regulated. But we're not on the gas mains here and there are no controls over LPG costs. Meade charges a ridiculous amount for LPG. Penelope and I get by here without it, just with electricity." The others nodded in agreement.

"And can you sell up and move out?"

There was the sound of bitter laughter around the table. "Oh yes, we're free to sell. Park homes get sold from time to time by estate agents. Meade gets 10% of the sale price."

"10% of the sale price?" Nick echoed.

"It's called commission, and the law says that the park owner is entitled to it regardless of how you find a buyer. You can't do anything about it. It means that lots of people find that they end up with less money than they paid in the first place. Bear in mind that these places don't really go up in value like ordinary houses do."

"OK," Nick was taking shorthand notes. This was information he hadn't known before, and he sensed there was a story to tell. The thought struck him that Martin Eveyard at the Observer might be prepared to commission a piece from him on this.

"Have any of the three of you thought of moving out?" he asked the room.

"Couldn't afford to move now," Jonathan Forrest responded. "And anyway it's hard to find buyers. Greensleeves has, what shall we say, something of a reputation locally. Anyone interested in a residential park home tends to find that out and pick another park."

"I see. So living here hasn't been quite as rewarding as you'd originally hoped?"

"The worst mistake of my life. Mr Meade saw me coming and stitched me up." The speaker this time was Richard Delano.

"Yes, fire away, Richard. Tell Mr Potterton your story," Peter Trelawney intervened.

Richard Delano's story seemed like it was going to be a long one. Nick allowed himself a sip of the beer.

Richard Delano had run a newsagents and convenience store in one of the old mill towns in Lancashire south of Preston. "Not a great business, but it ticked along nicely and my wife and I did all right. But the hours are long. 5.30 start to get the newspapers in and sorted, and then open till eight at night. I mean, it gets you down after a while. So when we both turned sixty we started thinking seriously about retiring." Nick felt that Richard Delano had told this part of his story before.

"My wife and I saw a retirement fair being advertised in a hotel near Chorley and went along. Greensleeves Park had a stall, and we started talking to the woman there. Never saw her again, I think Meade had employed her just for the event. She had the gift of the gab. Anyway, next thing we knew we were on a visit here, being given the guided tour and a glass of champagne for our efforts. Meade was canny: he made sure we only met residents he wanted us to meet. Some of the folk here, well, they haven't got a clue about the way things work and what's really going on and they still think Meade is the bee's knees."

He paused. "Meade took us back to the office and wanted us to sign up there and then. Some of the homes on the park he owned himself and he thought he could sell us one of these. But we were living above the shop, so we told him we would have to find a buyer for the business first."

Delano reached for his beer, and Nick took the opportunity to do the same. "So Meade told me he knew the answer. He'd wheedled out from me that I'd got a personal pension which I'd been carefully building up over the years. Ah, he said, take up your pension freedom rights. You're over 55, you've every right to cash it in. The pension firms don't like it because they miss out on all their fees and charges, but anyone with any sense has taken their pension pot by now and invested the money somewhere more lucrative. I know who you need to speak to. And he gave me a business card for a firm of financial advisers. Rosy Retirement. I should have known by the corny name that they'd be no good."

Delano, it transpired, had gone to Rosy Retirement for what they called a free initial consultation. The pension pot had been cashed in. The amount he realised wasn't enough by a long chalk to meet Meade's asking price, but the advisers had a suggestion here too. Delano took out a private loan to make up the difference, bought the park home and he and his wife made the move.

"Rosy Retirement is Mr Meade's own firm, isn't it?" Nick asked.

"Oh no, I don't think so. They told me they were independent," Delano replied. Nick went back to his note-taking.

Later things had unravelled. Out of the blue came a demand from the tax authorities to pay income tax on the bulk of the pension he'd realised. The newsagents business had failed to find a buyer, and he and his wife had been forced to bring in a manager to run it for them. The manager wasn't prepared to put in the hours. Turnover slumped.

"So to cut a long story short, I've lost my pension and we're broke," Richard Delano concluded. "So forgive me if I don't shed any tears over Mr Meade's fate." He paused for quite a long time.

"Actually, what's worse is that we're really lonely here. We're miles from the shops and we hardly ever go out in the evenings any more. I mean, it's been good to get to know Peter and Penelope, and Jonathan and his wife, and some of the others, but you can feel very trapped inside Greensleeves, as though the real world's happening somewhere else. You think it's going to be like being on holiday all the time but you very quickly discover that holidays are good precisely because they don't continue for ever."

There was silence in Rose Bower. Nick took this as a cue to make a move. He folded up his notebook and finished his beer.

"Thank you Richard, and thank you Peter and Jonathan too. And you, Penelope" (this to a figure in the recesses of the home). He checked with them that he had their mobile numbers, and then double-checked that he had their names spelled right. "Oh please don't use our real names in any article," Jonathan implored him. "Mr Meade will make our lives hell."

Mr Meade, Nick felt like replying, is currently not in a position to do any such thing. But he stayed silent, thanked his hosts again and pulled the front door closed behind him. Now for the second instalment of his Greensleeves social evening, he thought to himself. Now for the employees' stories. He left his car where it was and made his way up the road on foot, towards the lights of the pub.

9.

The over-milky and over-weak cappuccinos had been drunk and Adam had hurried away from the café in Keswick in order not to be late for his work. Geoff Handley, waiting behind for the bill to arrive, had taken the decision not to return down the M6 to his own work. Just occasionally he needed to enjoy the benefits which could come from running his own business, he told himself.

He put a call through to his PA who worked in the restored eighteenth-century barn complex in the Forest of Bowland which, some years back, he had chosen as the base for Geoff Handley Associates. He told her not to expect him back that afternoon and asked her to find and book him a room for the night in a decent country hotel. Somewhere near Keswick with a good restaurant and a swimming pool, he had added.

She'd rung back ten minutes later, and fifteen minutes after that his satnav had delivered him to the front door of a stone-built hotel set in pleasant lawns with gardens dropping down to Derwentwater below. He brought in from the Lexus an overnight bag he had packed earlier in the day, on a just-in-case basis.

The room he had been given had, generally, been well decorated and furnished. As always this was the first thing he checked when he was in a hotel. There was a big Victorian double bed in dark oak, repro but good repro, in the centre of the room, the bed covered with a tasteful cream bed-throw. Around the walls was period oak furniture to match: a well-proportioned chest of drawers, a wardrobe and a fine writing desk. The curtains had been selected well, too: it was a design which Handley couldn't immediately place but which was broadly in the arts-and-crafts style. Sanderson perhaps, although he didn't think so.

Only the carpet was disappointing. It was a lack-lustre affair in a sort of nondescript light pink. Unlike the rest of the room the carpet was shouting out the message 'provincial hotel room'.

Geoff sighed. Perhaps when he eventually retired and sold his business he might be able to walk into a hotel room without feeling the urge to appraise it professionally. He wondered whether the hotel owners here had undertaken the furnishing themselves or whether they'd gone to a design consultancy. Geoff knew that his own firm hadn't been offered the contract, but then increasingly he had been moving away from the upmarket English country clubs and country hotels which had once been the mainstay of his business. Now GHA was increasingly in demand for commissions abroad. Geoff himself had overseen a valuable contract in one of the Grenadine islands in the Caribbean, furnishing and fitting out an exclusive holiday hotel and spa, and there were similar commissions coming in for a safari lodge in Kenya and for a small chain of boutique hotels in Sri Lanka. Geoff himself had over the past few years become one of the best-known figures in his line of work, helped perhaps by the little bit of television exposure he'd received from a series he'd worked with for BBC2.

Actually, Geoff Handley decided, there was a lot just right about this hotel, including the large swimming pool in an annexe at the back with windows looking out over the lakeside gardens. It was late afternoon and the pool was deserted. Having already changed in his room into his swimming shorts (a print design from an upmarket men's tailoring firm which he had worn for several years but which he still loved), he slipped off the hotel towelling dressing gown and dived into the deep end. He was not particularly sporty and had always been hopeless at school games, but one thing he could do well was swim.

He began with a few lengths breast-stroke to warm up, and then changed to front crawl, driving himself up and down the pool. He loved the sense of power and physicality he had when swimming. The time slipped by. He had time to think through the events of the day.

Adam Meade. Had he liked Adam? Yes, he thought that he had. The young man had something of the looks of his father, and something of the same directness in the way he spoke to you. He was still young of course – 21, Richard had once told him – but clearly beginning to make his own way in life.

Had the meeting gone as he'd hoped? To an extent. Geoff was sorry in hindsight that he'd used subterfuge to arrange things. Having met Adam he'd wished he'd just made contact himself without involving Josie. Still, even in the twenty-first century you sometimes found yourself having to be less upfront about your sexuality than you'd want to be, and Geoff had not known at that stage how Adam would react. The big priority for him had been to ensure that the meeting with Adam could happen. And it had. And Adam now had his phone number and email address.

Geoff hoped that Adam would use them. At the end of their conversation in the cafe, Geoff had moved the conversation round to Greensleeves. Geoff had mentioned that he'd made a loan to Richard, although he hadn't let on quite how much he'd advanced. In hindsight it was probably a foolish investment, made with the heart and not the head.

Geoff Handley changed strokes, slowly propelling himself through the water on his back. There was just one aspect to the encounter with Adam about which, in hindsight, he felt uncomfortable. There had been one thing he'd said which wasn't precisely a lie, but on the other hand wasn't necessarily the full unvarnished truth. He'd described himself as Richard Meade's boyfriend. Did it matter? In the circumstances, probably not.

Thursday

1.

It was publication day for the *Cumbrian Enquirer*. Once upon a time the paper had had its own printing presses, together with a team of compositors wielding the individual hot metal letters of text ready to create the moulds from which the paper was produced. Not any more. These days the *Enquirer* used a contract printer over in Newcastle, the files for the pages being downloaded electronically every Wednesday evening and the finished paper, ready bundled, being trucked back along the A69 very early on Thursday morning and then taken to Penrith where a fleet of smaller vans was ready to undertake the local distribution. The system was well-honed and normally the week's *Cumbrian Enquirer* could be relied upon to be in the newsagents and shops by seven in the morning, if not earlier.

George Mulholland drove to his local newsagents in Cockermouth on his way to work that morning. He grimaced to himself when he saw the *Enquirer*'s front page. *The Body in the Bog – was it Murder?* This was the question he had been asking himself ever since he was called from home late on Sunday afternoon, and his difficulty was that it was a question for which he still didn't have a satisfactory answer. He read the story slowly and deliberately before he left for the drive to Whitehaven. Molly's article, not least the revelation that Meade's body was stripped half-naked, would start hares running among the other local media. His press conference later that morning would be well attended.

He had arranged a preparatory briefing meeting for 8.30am. DS Kate Morgan, the office manager for the enquiry, was already waiting for him when he arrived at eight.

"Media guys all ready for later on," she said. "Sir – they are asking if we know yet what the line will be. I mean, whether we're saying it could be murder."

"Unexplained death," Mulholland replied. "Tragic event, our thoughts with the family. Police following up all leads of enquiry, nothing ruled out at this stage. Appeal to the public for any information they hold. That's the plan."

Kate Morgan offered her boss a sheaf of papers. "Here's the transcript of the interview with Mr Rugglesdon which Sergeant Chambers did yesterday. I prevailed on one of the civilian staff to type it up first thing. Chambers is already here, by the way, if you need her."

"OK. I'll read it straightaway. Tell her to come in in five minutes."

Mulholland eased himself into his office chair and started reading. By the time a knock came at the door he was sitting pensively gazing at the wall, the papers strewn across the desk.

"Come in," he said. Chrissy Chambers, tidy in her uniform, appeared at the door.

"Well, Sergeant. Mr Rugglesdon has been a silly boy, hasn't he? All for a hundred pounds. Why are human beings so idiotic?"

Chambers made as if to reply but Mulholland waved her silent. "Good interview. Good work, Chrissy," he went on.

It was, Chambers realised, the first time he had used her first name. It was an encouraging sign that she was now considered to be one of the team. But it came just at the time when she felt she least deserved any compliments.

"Thank you sir, but I'm afraid I failed to ask Rugglesdon the one question I should have done." She reported briefly on the diversion she and PC Whittaker had made on the journey back, the one which had taken them to Wasdale Head.

"No mobile phone signal?" Mulholland enquired, repeating back what she had said.

"None at all. Of course, I should have thought of this right from the start. It explains, among other things, the lack of phone data from the network operator after around 11.30pm on Saturday night."

"It does. Except that Rugglesdon said that the reason why Meade couldn't climb Scafell Pike was because he was still on the phone at about one o'clock. Your thoughts?"

"A satellite phone maybe would work up there. It seems pretty unlikely that Meade would have one, but I can get it checked out. The only alternative, I guess, is that Rugglesdon is telling lies."

"Didn't some of Meade's staff also say that he was on his mobile phone?"

"Yes, sir, they did. Or at least, one of them did, the woman called Monica Roughlee."

"All right, we'll talk to her again. And we'll get Rugglesdon in. Get someone at the Kendal station to bring him over here this time, I can't spare you for a second sight-seeing jaunt round the Lake

District." He paused momentarily. "But first I want to focus on the press conference. Team briefing in ten minutes."

"Yes, sir."

Mulholland turned back to the papers on his desk. Chrissy Chambers slipped from the room.

2.

Nick Potterton's day started at seven o'clock with stale cornflakes and a small glass of very dilute orange juice. Forewarned by this of what was likely to follow he turned down the offer of a full English breakfast and instead went straight on to toast and marmalade, the toast arriving white and cold and the marmalade coming served in a tiny glass dish.

This was the Breakfast part of the B&B package for which he had agreed the night before to pay £70. The Bed part was a single room up in the rafters of a guest house, with a small dormer window, a small TV and a very small bed with an uncomfortable mattress. Oh, the delights of the English hospitality industry.

He was in Lytham, or was it St Anne's? This was supposed to be the classier part of the Blackpool coastline, away from all the Kiss-me-quick razzmatazz and tourist tat of Blackpool itself. Still, he couldn't complain. He'd found a bed for the night at half past nine the previous evening, and he'd found a taxi to fetch him from the Traveller's Rest and take him there. All he had to do was to find a taxi now to take him back. His car was still at Greensleeves and he needed to be the other side of Morecambe Bay as quickly as possible, to get ready for the morning shift on the *Enquirer*.

Peggy and Monica and the young man called Peter had been in the Traveller's Rest bar when he had finally got there, Peggy and Monica with glasses of white wine and Peter with a pint of Thwaites. Nick's impression was that they were already several rounds of drinks ahead of him. He ordered a pint and sat down to join them.

"At last! We thought you'd stood us up." Monica was showing signs of the effects of the alcohol.

"Be nice to him, Monica. He's just spent the first part of the evening with dreary Mr Trelawney." This was Peter's riposte.

"Peter Trelawney's not so bad. Meade didn't like him, but then Meade didn't like anyone," said Peggy. Nick noticed that she had dropped the 'Mr' in Mr Meade. The boss's power was slipping away.

"Anyway, everything is fixed now." (Monica again). "We've agreed that we'll take over Greensleeves and run it ourselves, just like the weasels in Toad Hall. Peggy will be the managing director, I will be chief administrative officer and Peter will be the guy who sorts out the sewage."

"That's *not* what we agreed I'd do," Peter piped up. "Anyway, what about Jack?"

"Jack deserves promotion. We'll make him operations director. He can direct you as you sort out the sewage."

Peggy tittered. "Mr Potterton's not here to listen to our chatter. He's got sensible questions to ask us."

Nick reflected that, given the circumstances, his sensible questions were unlikely to attract many sensible answers. He pondered passing his pint untouched to Peter and getting straight on the road. But he was tired, the pub was warm and he was also very hungry. "What sort of food do they do here?" he asked.

And, a little later, as he tackled a warm chicken Caesar, Nick decided he'd made the right decision. The conversation took a different turn. Nick tuned back in to what was being said.

"I turned him down, of course. He was claiming that he wanted to institute an employee share-ownership scheme, but I think he was short of the readies and thought his staff could help him out," Peggy was saying.

"Oh, he never asked me," Monica said.

"Maybe it was only some of the staff. Meade claimed there were tax advantages for us with his proposal but I wasn't convinced. He said the money for the Greensleeves shares would simply be taken each month from our pay but I wanted the cash, not some share certificate. God knows, he was paying us little enough anyway."

"Did anyone take up his offer, do you think?" asked Monica.

"I know for a fact that nobody in the office did. I suppose Jack Higgins might have agreed."

"Jack is the last person who'd be inclined to help Meade out."

"Yes, but have you noticed how grumpy he has been recently?"

"Jack's always been bad-tempered."

"But he has now reached an altogether higher plane of bad-temperedness," Peggy replied.

Nick intervened. "So apart from Mr Meade and just possibly Mr Higgins, who else held Greensleeves' shares?" he asked.

"Nobody's sure, although there's been talk of some sort of family trust. For his two sons, you know. And then there's Meade's business associates. There was a man called Geoff who was around a lot some weeks back. Word had it that he became a shareholder too," Peggy said.

"Any idea of his surname?" Nick asked.

Peggy shrugged.

"Whoever he was, he wangled his way out of the Three Peaks weekend," Monica chipped in. Her blisters were still bloody and raw she went on, this comment being addressed particularly to Nick.

And at this point the conversation had veered off in another direction once more. Nick had gone to the bar to buy drinks and at the same time had asked whether the Traveller's Rest had a spare room for the night. They hadn't, but between the bar staff and the regulars at the bar they'd found him a room at the guest house on the coast.

And here now, appearing through the windows of the taxi, was the Traveller's Rest once again. The taxi pulled up at the gates of Greensleeves and Nick reached for his money while at the same time pulling out his car keys. It was a quarter to eight. Good. Provided the motorways were clear he'd have time to get back home to Grasmere, to change out of the previous day's clothes. And to brush his teeth. The taste of the acidic marmalade from the B&B breakfast was still lingering in his mouth.

That was the plan. It's good to have plans, because where would we be without them? However, plans sometimes end up being changed.

Nick took the A591 from the M6 and drove through Windermere and Ambleside before turning off the main Keswick road just north of the village of Grasmere. The lane where he lived was a quiet area, well away from Grasmere's village centre where the tourists foregathered. His place was the middle of a small terrace of three houses built of Cumbrian stone and slate, set by themselves with fine views over the fells.

The front door was unlocked. Nick had never had a Yale lock fitted for the door, making do with the single deadlock which had been there when he first moved in. Sometimes he didn't bother with locking this, particularly when he was off for a short early morning run on the fells and didn't want to have to take keys. On the other hand, he did usually lock the house securely when he went off to work. He was almost certain he'd done so the day before. He was getting absent-minded as well as careless, he told himself.

Inside everything was as he'd left it. There was washing up left in the kitchen going back to his Monday evening pasta meal as well as several days' unopened mail on one of the living room chairs. God, his single lifestyle was causing standards to slip. He must get on top of the housework.

But something wasn't right. The fact that the front door was unlocked was niggling him and Nick had a sudden sixth sense that someone had been in his house since he was last there. He could almost sense their presence. Shit, a burglary. What had he lost?

He looked around. The television hadn't been touched and his expensive digital SLR camera was still there. He bounded up the stairs: no obvious sign of anything missing from the spare room which he used as his office. The PC was in place, along with the external hard-drive he used for back-ups. His tablet was there too. Tablets were eminently nickable, so perhaps he had been mistaken to think there had been an intruder. All seemed well. Still, he'd have to be more sensible about locking the place up in the future, he said to himself.

He looked at the research papers for his nuclear power book, which were spread out as usual on the spare room bed and on the floor. And then he saw it: a small round badge with a smiling sun and the legend *Nuclear? No gràcies* carefully placed on the top of one of the piles of papers. The badge dated back to the 1980s, and was one of a host of similar anti-nuclear badges produced at the time, in almost all the languages you could think of. This one was in Catalan, the language Ana spoke and had tried to teach Nick when they'd started living together. The badge came later. It had been a jokey present from his daughter Rosa who had found it in a second-hand shop in Barcelona and had given it to her father when he'd first got the book commission. He'd kept it, along with a stack of old reporters' notebooks and pencils, deep in one of his desk drawers. He'd not seen it for ages.

So there had been someone in his office, someone who had spurned his tablet and his camera but who had had sufficient time to rummage in his office, to unearth the badge and to leave it – why? – as a curious sort of calling card. He thought back to Tuesday morning, when he had last worked on the book, when he'd rung the Professor and Greenpeace International and then told his publisher that the text was nearly complete. Was it possible, could it be conceivable, that somebody was so keen to get hold of his book that they simply weren't prepared to wait like everyone else for publication day? Obtaining a copy of the text from his PC would have been the work of a moment, Nick thought ruefully.

What was the right thing to do at moments like this? He pondered ringing 999 but in the end rang the non-emergency police number. A bored-sounding woman, presumably a civilian working for the police, eventually answered. Nick told her that he was reporting a burglary, but the answers he provided to the questions she started to go through sounded – he had to admit – all too implausible. No, nothing taken. No, no sign of forced entry. Yes, through the front door, and it was just conceivable the front door had been left unlocked anyway. No, only an old badge deliberately moved.

Nick had imagined that an appropriate first step would be for a scene of crime officer to be sent round to check the badge, and his office papers, for fingerprints. But by the end of the call, he was not surprised when the woman laconically terminated the conversation. The police might call him back – but he would appreciate how busy the police were these days. No, no crime number, because it was not clear that a crime had been committed. Goodbye.

More shaken than he expected, he filled the kettle and primed the small cafetière with coffee. Another five minutes more, and he'd be ready to head to the *Enquirer*. He'd be very late, but Molly would understand.

He had just taken the first sip of his drink when his mobile rang. He recognised the number: it was Pat, the mountain rescue team's President.

"Hello, Pat," he said in answering. "Not a call-out, I hope?"

"No, Nick, Listen, I'm really sorry I've got to make this call. You've let me down badly."

"Sorry?"

"You've broken your word." This was Pat talking to him in a way he'd never experienced before. "I defended the idea of having you in the team when some people said it wasn't appropriate, but that was on the strict understanding you'd never write about mountain rescue matters in the press."

"Yes, that's what we agreed, and I haven't."

"Come on, do me a favour. I can read, you know. Front page of today's *Enquirer*, Body in the Bog, and whose name is underneath the story? A certain Nick Potterton. You were with the team on the search on Sunday and you wrote it up on Monday."

"Pat, I can see what you're thinking but believe me, that's not what happened..."

Pat interrupted him. "I'm sorry, Nick. I'm going to refer your membership to the next committee. But in the meantime, I have to tell you that I'm suspending you. Don't call in to the base. I'll need your ID back, but you can post it."

She rang off. Nick took a deep breath, and reached for the mug.

The phone rang a second time. It was a familiar London voice.

"Nick, nice work," Martin Eveyard began. "Just a couple of minor queries being raised by the subs. Have you got a moment?"

Nick pulled himself together and thought back to the Three Peaks piece he had filed to the Observer the day before. The sub-editors' queries were indeed minor, and he had the information Martin was asking for.

"Martin, before you go, I've got another story here which I think might interest you."

"Go on."

Nick briefly spelled out how he envisaged a story about the retirement park industry. Parliament might have tried to prevent bad practice, but there was still scope for abuse. Older people, particularly those without deep pockets, were the people most at risk. Some people might love their retirement park home, but for others it could be a trap. Nick described briefly what he'd gleaned from his visits to Greensleeves.

The other end of the phone was quiet. "Very interesting, Nick, but you know, I don't think it's quite right for us. And I'd be worried about bringing Mr Meade into another story so quickly. Actually, my freelance budget is almost gone at the moment anyway. I'll have to let you take this elsewhere. But keep in touch."

The call ended and Nick sighed. The coffee was now cold. He had just been told that he had effectively spent the last few days driving backwards and forwards between the Lake District and a residential park near Blackpool for no good reason at all. Had he lost his professional grasp of what made a good story, he asked himself? Was Martin's comment about his budget just an excuse or had another of Nick's potential clients joined the *Enquirer* in deciding to cut back on freelance contributors? His ability to earn even a half-way decent income from the job he loved was slipping away week by week.

It was already nearly ten o'clock. He was now seriously late for work, but the *Enquirer*'s office suddenly felt like the last place he wanted to be. He had just suffered a disturbingly strange burglary, he'd been sacked from mountain rescue and had his pitch to the Observer rejected. Maybe he'd jack it all in, text Molly and resign, get his running kit on and head straight out for a day in the hills. Fairfield. Helvellyn, why not?

The phone rang a third time.

"Ooh, Nick, sorry to trouble you but I thought you were working with us today?"

It was the woman called Petra who handled the switchboard at the *Enquirer*.

"I am, Petra. I'm on my way. It's turning into a difficult morning."

"OK, but I've just had a phone call through. It's from a man who called himself Rob Ruggleston, and he was desperate to talk to Molly."

"Rug Rugglesdon," Nick corrected.

"Molly's at the police conference and I can't reach her but I think someone needs to ring him back. He's got something important to tell us, he says. Can you ring him?"

"I'll do it from here straightaway," Nick replied.

Rug Rugglesdon sounded like a man on the brink of a breakdown.

"I've just seen your front page," he said. "I'd no idea there was any suggestion of murder. I think… I think I may have misled the police without meaning to," he started.

Nick made encouraging noises.

"The police interviewed me yesterday. It was horrible, it went on for hours. I told them everything I knew. There was just one question where perhaps I got my answer wrong."

"Go on."

"I told them Mr Meade was on his mobile phone when we started off for Scafell Pike."

"And wasn't he?"

"No. He was pretending to talk to somebody. Mind you, he was pretty convincing. I don't think anyone else realised."

"I see. Why didn't you tell this to the police, Mr Rugglesdon?"

"Because… Because, I know this is stupid, but Mr Meade had told me beforehand that I absolutely mustn't tell anyone. When he first arranged for me to be the guide, that is."

"Mr Meade arranged with you beforehand that he would pretend to be on his phone at Wasdale Head, so he wouldn't have to go up Scafell Pike?" Nick enquired incredulously. "Didn't he fancy a clamber up another mountain?"

"It wasn't that. He said he'd got to meet a business contact, and this was the only time he could do it."

"At one in the morning in Wasdale?"

"That's what he said. He said he'd only be fifteen minutes or so. He said he'd catch us up. And he told me that I had to keep this arrangement private, so I did. Even when the police asked me. Mr Meade could be very persuasive."

"Obviously."

"What should I do?"

"Mr Rugglesdon I'm a journalist and I don't give advice. But it sounds to me that if you don't tell the police now everything you know you'll be even deeper in the shit."

"I thought so too. I'll ring the police now."

"You might want to get yourself a solicitor first."

"But I really haven't done anything wrong." The tone was plaintive.

"Whatever you think is best." Nick had been taking shorthand notes during the conversation. This looked remarkably as though it might be next week's front page lead too. Perhaps he wouldn't resign from the *Enquirer* straight away.

He took his coffee mug over to the sink and washed it, leaving the rest of the dirty washing-up untouched. Work was calling. But at that moment there was a rap at his front door.

"Come in, it's open," he called. It would be one of his neighbours. Hardly anyone else called at this time of day.

The rapping continued. Nick sighed, and went to open the door. Outside were two young uniformed police officers, one woman and one man.

"Mr Potterton, Mr Nick Potterton?" said the woman.

"Yes, that's right. God, you've been quick," Nick said. "I must confess that I thought you might not bother to attend. I appreciate my case isn't a usual one."

Nick saw the two officers exchange glances.

"Come in. You'll want to see the badge. That's the only proof of anything untoward."

"Mr Potterton," (this was the woman officer again), "we are here as part of our investigation into the death of Mr Richard Meade. We need to ask you some questions."

"Meade? Ah I see, you'd still better come in."

"If you don't mind sir, we will need to ask you to accompany us to the police station."

"Yes but not now. I'm late for work as it is."

"I understand the inconvenience, sir, but I must ask you to come with us now. The patrol car is outside waiting."

And, with just the time to lock his front door carefully, Nick found himself leaving his house with his two assiduous escorts.

"There you are, sir, sit in the back if you don't mind," said the male officer.

The car drove off.

3.

Molly couldn't quite put her finger on it, but her relationship with George Mulholland had somehow become more difficult. Perhaps it was his promotion up another rung on the police ladder that had made the difference. He was now more cautious with her. He was, bluntly, less fun.

On the surface, nothing had changed. After the press conference – which had been something of a waste of time in Molly's opinion – she'd lingered behind. George had, as she'd expected, come up to her, offering the usual compliments he undoubtedly offered all his lady acquaintances. "In these modern times I am careful with what I say, but I trust it would not offend political correctness to say how gorgeous you are looking this morning," was how he put it. Molly had laughed.

They had gone out to a sandwich bar just round the corner from the Whitehaven police station, where George bought Molly a cappuccino.

"So, Molly, I wonder what front page surprise you have in store for me next week," he began.

"I wonder, too," Molly had replied. "It's only Thursday. I've only just sent this week's paper to the press."

"…Because your old friend DCI Mulholland here always reads your paper avidly to see if you can solve any of his crimes for him."

"Thank you, George, but I seem to remember that you're more than capable of solving your own cases. Although I do get just a hint that Mr Meade is a slightly trickier case for you than usual."

"Ah well, it all comes down to patience in detective work, and I've learned how to be more patient as I've got older. You journalists wouldn't understand that, though. Always a rush to the next deadline."

Molly looked at George Mulholland over her coffee cup. It was true, he was looking older.

"Any thoughts of retirement soon, George? I thought you coppers could take your pension ridiculously early."

"Ah, they're changing the rules to try to make us stay on to sixty and frankly that will suit me. I'm not ready yet to put my feet up. Although –"

He abruptly stopped. All the police forces, including the Cumbrian one, were having to make do with major budget reductions at the moment. Staff numbers were falling. Molly suddenly had a thought that George might be fighting to keep his job. Was that why he had recently seemed more tetchy?

"And what about the *Enquirer*? All hunky-dory at your work?"

"Not too bad, thanks," Molly lied. "All set for the digital age. Give us a few more months and you'll be reading our news every week on your tablet. Or maybe on your watch."

"Hmm, my wristwatch is still very much of the traditional variety, and all the better for that. Tell me, how is your young newshound Potterton these days? Bringing in the scoops?"

Molly laughed. "Are you trying to pump me to find out who our contacts were on the Meade story?"

"Heaven forfend," Mulholland replied. "Although don't let me stop you telling me."

"George, believe me, I know for a fact that any information from me wouldn't help your enquiry. So, sorry, journalistic ethics apply." She paused. "Still, Meade is turning out to be a pretty rum sort of character, isn't he? Under the do-goody charity fundraising front, he seems to have been engaged in some curious business dealings."

"Ah, Molly, now in turn you are trying to pump me. You're too transparent, I'm afraid."

Molly laughed. "All right, I'll leave it there. Don't forget the offer of a pint some time though."

"The prospect remains a delightful one and I am sure you will do me the honour of allowing me to buy the drinks. But sadly the world is not yet perfect and I must return to my over-heated little police room." He finished his coffee and they both got up.

"Molly, ring me on my home mobile if you want to. I'm busy, but never too busy to talk," he added almost under his voice as they left.

"All right, George," Molly smiled. "Tell you what: I'll race you to the solution of the Meade case. Whoever wins buys the drinks."

4.

Thursdays were always busy. Adam Meade had been on the breakfast shift, finally getting the last of the food dispatched to the resident guests and the kitchen cleaned down around ten. He'd gone back briefly to his room, thought things through, and finally sent a text. "Geoff," it read. "Have been thinking about what you said. Not sure, but maybe we should meet again. Could drive and meet you somewhere." He signed off with his full name: "Adam Meade."

And then, almost immediately, it was time to get back to work. The lunch trade in the hotel was gradually picking up as the summer holiday season in Keswick began to get under way. Adam put on his chef's whites for the second time that day and reported to the kitchen. He had decided not to tell Chef or any of the others of his father's death. He felt that they would have felt the need to make sympathetic noises but would also have felt that he was claiming special favours. He wanted to be judged at work just by how he performed. Anyway, he didn't know any of them particularly well.

It was after things had wound down, well after half past two, and he was making his way back through the hotel's reception area that he saw the copy of the *Cumbrian Enquirer*, put out for guests to browse. He knew at once that the front page story was about his father. Stupid, he'd never even thought that the media might be going to pick up on the story.

But what he found himself gazing at with dull incomprehension was the headline.

THE BODY IN THE BOG

– WAS IT MURDER?

Murder! He knew of course that the Plods were doing an investigation – he had met one of the detectives in charge when he and his mother had had to identify his father's body on Tuesday morning – but until that moment nobody had suggested to him that they could be treating his dad's death as a potential case of murder. He read with disbelief the text below the headline. The body, according to the *Enquirer*'s reporters, had been found almost without clothes. In a state of semi-undress, naked to the waist, that was what the paper was claiming. Nothing he had been told up to now had prepared him for this bit of news.

Adam went to his room. He had become mixed up, he suddenly realised, with something incomprehensible, something which could turn his life upside-down.

What could he do? He tried putting calls through to his brother and then to his mother, but neither were picking up their phones. Dan would be at college and his mother would be working. Maybe that was for the better. What would he have said to them which wouldn't have made them even more upset and more anxious for him?

He sat on his bed, thinking long and hard at what the last few days meant, and what he should do. He toyed with the idea of ringing the police, but couldn't bring himself to make the call. In the end he punched another set of numbers into his mobile.

The call was received by the *Enquirer*'s switchboard operator. "Hello," said the caller. "You don't know me but I'm ringing about your front page article in the paper today. My name's Adam Meade and I'm Richard Meade's son."

5.

George Mulholland's office was as malodorous as ever. He was behind his desk. At his side was detective sergeant Kate Morgan, the enquiry's office manager, and around him were sitting the more senior members of the investigation team. Sergeant Chrissy Chambers, to her pleasure and slight surprise, had been invited too.

"All right, before we start, an update. Mr Rupert Rugglesdon or Rug as he prefers to call himself contacted us by phone this morning while I was dealing with the media. He has admitted that he lied yesterday when being interviewed by Sergeant Chambers here." Mulholland looked across to where Chrissy Chambers was sitting. "Rugglesdon now says that he was privy to a prior arrangement with Meade which would enable Meade to avoid the Scafell Pike climb on Sunday morning in order to meet a business acquaintance. At one in the morning. I know it sounds implausible but that is what Rugglesdon is claiming. I intend to follow this up myself. In the meantime, we have arrested him under Section 5 (2) of the 1967 Act. It'll do at least as an interim measure. He's been bailed. Now to the business in hand. Malcolm, tell us all you know of Richard Meade's business interests," Mulholland began.

The man he was addressing was, like all the room except Chrissy Chambers, in plain clothes. Malcolm Macdonald, a police specialist in fraud and business crime, was normally based in Carlisle but had been brought in to work on the Meade case on Tuesday.

He began briskly. "Mr Meade was effectively the owner of Greensleeves Residential Park," he began. "The legal structure's complicated and I'll come back to that, but let's start with the basics. Meade's got fifty-four residential units who pay a monthly pitch fee, so that's 54 times £185 or in other words an annual income of around £120,000. On top of that he benefits from the 10% sale commission when units are sold, and in some years this can be a very valuable income generator. For example if one in ten units are sold in any one year that amounts to another £60,000 or so. Seven of the units are owned directly by Meade and are tenanted rather than owner-occupied, so the rent from the tenants comes to him. There are some incidental sources of income as well: commission from the finance companies when people buy their homes with a loan, for example. We're talking of a turnover of something a little over a quarter of a million."

Chrissy Chambers noticed that Malcolm Macdonald had reverted to talking about Meade in the present tense.

"Expenditure?" interjected Mulholland.

Malcolm Macdonald looked down at the big stack of paper in front of him, which included several years' worth of duplicate bank statements. "Staff wages are the major item. Seven employees, plus Meade himself of course. Four of the staff are on the minimum wage, and he also uses zero contracts a lot. I'd say he certainly gets his money's worth from them. Then there are other items of expenditure. Site insurance, various licensing fees from the local authority, solicitors' and accountants' charges. The business should certainly wash its face, but frankly we're not talking massive profits. Meade was a minnow in the industry beside the major companies, some of which these days can own thirty or forty separate residential parks. But he didn't necessarily see himself as a minnow. He had a pretty lavish lifestyle for the size of the business he ran."

"He had debts?"

"Residential parks went through a sticky period a few years back when there were very few people buying and selling units, and Greensleeves was no exception. Meade took out a business loan five years ago secured on the assets. Basically a mortgage loan, if you like. He's been struggling to service the interest payments. I know that the finance company has the lawyers involved already."

"How did Meade come to own Greensleeves? Did he start it himself?"

"No, it began in the 1950s as a holiday caravan site and basically just took off from there. The planning laws were pretty lax back then. By the 1990s it was being run as a private business and the owner put it up for sale when he retired. Meade had made money when he was in his twenties trading motors and in 2002 he and a business associate called Jack Higgins bought Greensleeves. Four years later he bought out Higgins' share. I've looked at the deal Meade struck then, and frankly I suspect Higgins now regrets what he agreed to. He ended up as one of Meade's employees. Not to put it too finely, Meade fucked him over."

"Higgins wasn't one of the happy little staff party on the Three Peaks trip, was he? At Wasdale Head that evening?" Mulholland asked.

"No, sir," replied Kate Morgan. "He was the one employee who wasn't there. Nobody's interviewed him yet."

"We'll remedy that. Sergeant Chambers, one for you. Find out why he didn't fancy a weekend of mountaineering. Find out in particular what he was doing last Saturday night. Or claimed he was doing. Interview him this afternoon and take PC Whittaker if she's available. Oh, and talk as well to that woman at the caravan park who also claimed to have seen Meade speaking on his mobile."

Chambers nodded. "Monica Roughlee. OK, understood."

Malcolm Macdonald continued. "Things are complicated by the fact that Meade separated the legal ownership of the land from the management of the park and he also was clearly trying to minimise his tax bill by having a holding company in the Isle of Man, but to simplify things all you need to know is that Meade ensured that he stayed in control."

"His family?" Mulholland asked.

"He's divorced. There's a family trust which gives his two sons a quarter each of Greensleeves when they reach eighteen. One is still under age but the other, Adam, is 21 and is registered at Companies House as a Greensleeves director. I wonder if he knows what he's let himself in for."

"Adam Meade undertook the body identification with his mother on Monday. I gather he works in a hotel or a restaurant of some kind, in Keswick." Mulholland turned to the detective sergeant who had been with him in Wasdale Head on Sunday afternoon. "We need to talk to him properly, Patrick. See to this please."

"Meade was not just in debt to the finance company. He was also very late with corporation tax and VAT on the business, and on his own income tax. Another month or so and the business might have been a goner," Malcolm Macdonald continued.

"Meade would have known this when he planned the Three Peaks," Mulholland responded. "This enquiry hasn't ruled out the possibility that he took his own life."

"Indeed, sir, although Meade was given a respite. He had someone who was prepared to help a friend in need."

"Meaning?" This was Mulholland again.

"He was lent, or maybe given, £60,000 by a man called Geoff Handley. Handley is an interior designer, quite well known. I've not found any paperwork to explain the basis of the money, but the payment went out of Handley's bank account and into Meade's a little earlier this year."

"Business associate?"

"Maybe something more. Handley's emails to Meade are pretty personal. The implication has to be that they were lovers."

There was a moment of silence around the table.

"I see," said Mulholland eventually. "This could explain why we've been able to track down several of Meade's former girlfriends from times past but nobody who admits to a more recent relationship. Any other evidence that Meade buttered his bread on both sides?"

Kate Morgan responded by shaking her head. "Bisexual? No other evidence yet."

"I want Mr Handley brought in. And a DNA sample off him. Just in case he and Meade had decided to share some night-time pranks up in the mountains." Mulholland paused. "Four days gone already! We should have known this on Monday."

"Yes, sir," Morgan replied.

"All right, thank you Malcolm. Stay behind, will you, I want to go through the details of the paperwork you've got there. The rest of you are dismissed. Chins up, everyone, we're making good progress."

6.

Nick had had to endure a tedious hour or so in the company of the Cumbrian police, or at least two of their number, before he'd been allowed to go on his way. He'd been treated scrupulously politely, but the police were clearly trying to find out his sources for the Meade story. In reality he had little enough that he could have told them but in any case he wasn't about to break the journalists' code of confidentiality towards sources. After all, there had been cases where journos had risked prison rather than break what was a fundamental aspect of the way journalism was done in Britain.

There was just one aspect of the police questioning where Nick had felt uncomfortable.

"Mr Potterton," the female officer had asked him. "You were seen by a police officer late on Monday morning in running clothing, on a footpath north-west of Wast Water. Why did you choose to go running there at that time?"

"I had read the press release your force put out about the walker's body being discovered. I was interested to see the place," Nick had replied.

"Why that footpath in particular? The press release said only that the body had been found in the Wasdale area. But you knew exactly where it had been found. How was that?"

How, indeed, had he known? For a moment Nick had been genuinely uncertain before realising with embarrassment that it was only through the mountain rescue radio that he had heard talk of the casualty in the Pots of Ashness.

"I see," replied the policewoman tight-lipped, when he had admitted this fact.

Nick was forced to wonder if he had indeed deserved his suspension by Pat from the team.

Once away from the police, however, the day had begun to improve. He finally arrived at the *Enquirer* offices around half past two to find that Molly still hadn't got back from the police press conference in Whitehaven. Petra on the switchboard grabbed him as soon as he walked in.

"Nick," she said. "Just in time! I've got a man on the phone who's just rung in. He says that he's the son of, you know, the Body in the Bog, and he urgently wants to talk to us. I'll put him through to your extension."

Nick went to his desk and picked up his phone.

"Hello, Nick Potterton here."

"I'm Adam Meade. You said in your paper that my father may have been murdered."

"Yes, I was one of the reporters on that story."

"My dad told me just a short time ago that somebody might be out to do him in, and he told me to be careful for myself. In case, well, you know, in case of something similar. I thought you ought to know. I mean, right at the moment I'm feeling pretty frightened."

It was potentially a golden journalistic break-through, and Nick told himself that for moments like this he would endure any amount of tedious time spent in police stations. His pencil accelerated across his notebook.

"Adam, you've done the right thing in ringing. Tell you what, I suggest we meet up straightaway. Where are you ringing from?"

"No, I don't want to meet just at the moment."

"Adam, listen, I have to know that you're genuine. You could be anyone. You could be ringing me for a joke. If we meet, I'll know I can trust you."

"You can trust me. Honest. Ask me something to prove who I am."

Nick thought quickly. "All right, what's your father's middle name and where does your mother live?"

"He didn't have a middle name. And Mum lives in Barton-upon-Humber with my brother Dan." He gave the address and postcode. "There, now do you believe me?" he went on.

"OK, Adam, thank you. But what about you? Where are you living yourself? If you've seen our paper I imagine it's somewhere local."

"Never mind where I'm living. Well OK, just say it's somewhere in Cumbria. And please, I don't want to answer any more questions just at the moment."

"Adam, I understand you're anxious but please let's agree to meet to talk about this some more. Maybe tomorrow morning if today's no good."

"Maybe. I'll think about it."

"Listen, I'm going to give you my personal mobile number too, just in case you need to ring out of office hours. Ring at any time, about anything." Nick gave the numbers of his mobile phone slowly, twice over. "Got that?"

"Yes. I'm ringing off now."

"Adam, just a mo. Have you talked to the police yet? You should do, if you're personally at risk."

"Yeah, well that's up to me, isn't it. Anyway, I've got to go."

The line went dead. Nick sat for some time, peering down at his notebook. At that moment he heard the sound of Molly's arrival back.

"Richard Meade's son on the phone. He says his father told him someone might be out to get him. The son says he's frightened that someone's now going to try to get him as well."

Molly gave a gasp.

"Kosher?" All local papers had their fair share of nutty callers.

"I think so. I got him to tell me his mother's address, and he said" (Nick looked at his notes) "that she lives in somewhere called Barton-upon-Humber. We can check that out easily. Very useful to have that information."

"Yes. Where's he living?"

"He wouldn't say precisely. Somewhere in Cumbria, he said. I tried to persuade him to meet me, but I'm not sure I succeeded. Anyway, we've got his number now from the caller ID and he's got my mobile number too."

Nick paused. "Want to take this over, Molly?" It would be the editor's prerogative to follow up the lead, if she wanted.

"No, Nick, you carry on for now. I expect I can find a few more pounds in the freelance budget if I raid the petty cash tin. Where do you think this story's going?"

"Not sure, but I gleaned some useful information about Meade's business affairs when I was at Greensleeves yesterday evening. I spoke to one of the residents who more or less claimed that Meade had cheated him out of his pension money. Not quite the angle on Meade we ran on today's front page."

"That's true. Is this chap prepared to be quoted?"

"He seemed anxious but I don't think he's realised yet that Meade is not around any more to put the frighteners on him. Something else I picked up. Some of the staff told me that Meade had asked them to put some of their pay into the business."

"Did they agree?"

"No, or at least nobody except possibly the maintenance man."

"We need to get to the bottom of Meade's business, don't we? Perhaps a former Sunday Times journalist can work some magic, eh Nick?"

"Hang on, didn't you tell me when we had lunch to stop being an investigative journalist and to spend more time instead on dog shows?"

"Well, of course nothing beats a good dog show. But just this once I'll allow you to write about something else."

The phone extension rang again.

"Nick, is Molly with you?" It was Petra on the switchboard. "I've got a call for her."

"Yes, I'll put Molly on."

Molly took Nick's phone in her left hand, reaching as she did for Nick's notebook and turning to a blank page. "Molly Everett here."

Once more Teeline shorthand shapes appeared on the notebook. Molly's own contribution to the conversation was limited to some occasional interjections. The person at the other end was doing most of the talking.

"All right, Amanda. Thank you for letting me know," Molly said eventually.

She gave the phone back to Nick. "Rug Rugglesdon's mother. The police have arrested him," she said.

"Arrested him? What for?"

"For wasting police time. Well, at this stage at least. He's home now and in a pretty terrible state according to Amanda."

"I spoke to Rug this morning, it must have been before all this. He told me that Meade –"

The phone rang yet again. Nick stopped and picked the receiver up.

"Sorry Nick, another call." It was Petra. "For you this time."

"Hello, Nick, it's Monica," said the caller. "I'm really sorry to ring you again. There are two policewomen here at Greensleeves. They've taken over the office and have been in there talking to Jack Higgins. And then they say they want to interview me. Just me, nobody else. I'm really worried. What do I say to them?"

"Monica, I am afraid I am not your solicitor, but I'm sure you have nothing to fear if you tell the police everything you know."

"But why have they singled me out?"

"I'm sure they'll explain. Just be honest."

"And why Mr Higgins? It's been years since he sold his bit of the Greensleeves business to Mr Meade."

"Sorry? Jack Higgins used to be a co-owner of Greensleeves?"

"Yes, everyone knows that."

"Clearly, everyone except me."

There was a pause.

"Are you able to come back to see us? Please. And maybe be here when the police ask me their questions," Monica said plaintively.

Nick thought quickly. His priority was to be close at hand in case Adam Meade rang back and wanted to meet up. The father who was apparently murdered and the son who feared he was next in line: here was a scoop for the *Enquirer* like no other. On the other hand, it would be useful to talk again to Higgins, always assuming Higgins himself agreed and didn't reach for the lump hammer first.

Monica was still waiting for a reply. Even if Nick changed his plan and drove straight down to Greensleeves, there was a very strong chance that by the time he arrived the police would have finished interviewing Higgins who would have gone home. All in all, it would be much better to head down in the morning and catch Higgins at work.

"Monica, I'm sorry, I have things to do here. Much as I enjoyed last night I can't afford the time to spend another evening down in the Traveller's Rest. No promises, but I'll try to get down tomorrow."

A slight sob came down the phone in reply.

"You know how to reach me, Monica," Nick went on. He was about to add 'and you can ring me again when the Black Maria comes for you', before deciding that this was not the moment for levity.

"All right, Nick, thank you so much." The line went dead.

Molly put her head back round the door. "An admirer?"

"Normally in journalism we refer to them as contacts," Nick replied.

"It's been a long day," Molly responded. "You're looking tired."

"I want to forget today. I've never even mentioned to you the burglary I suffered this morning."

"No! At your Grasmere place?"

"Yes, a very peculiar burglar who seemed to be extremely interested in nuclear power and nothing else. I don't even want to think about it now. I'll tell you the whole saga tomorrow."

7.

Geoff Handley's PA had certainly found a good hotel for him when he'd rung her from Keswick. It not only had a decent swimming pool, it had also served up an excellent evening meal. The dinner wasn't precisely cheap (Geoff's bill had come in at over fifty pounds, although he had allowed himself two glasses of a good red wine), but the food was excellent. Handley enjoyed the satisfaction of making money from his business but he also enjoyed very much the pleasures that could come from spending it.

After a good night's sleep (firm mattress and good quality linen bedsheets, that box could be ticked), he decided to defer breakfast until after he had allowed himself the pleasure of a second visit to the swimming pool. As the evening before, he had the pool entirely to himself.

Swimming, or at least swimming on occasions like this where you didn't have to spend all your time avoiding splashy children and beginners, was when he did his thinking. The decision to leave his well-paid job with his old employer and start his own consultancy had been taken on holiday while swimming in the pool of an upmarket villa in Corfu. The time when he'd realised that he needed to move beyond the British market and extend his business overseas had come to him (he remembered the occasion well) in the heated outdoor pool of a country club somewhere near Ripon. The owner, one of his long-standing clients, had encouraged him to stay on and use the club's facilities after a long afternoon spent discussing a redesign job for the restaurant.

And the decision to invest in Greensleeves? Well of course that had been made in Richard Meade's own swimming pool one Sunday afternoon, after they had had sex together upstairs. There was an awful lot wrong with Meade's house in Handley's opinion. It was the epitome of bad taste, from the ugly electronic wrought iron gates which held back the plebs to the swanky gold taps in the ridiculously large walk-in shower room. But the pool was the house's redeeming feature – well, that and of course the fact that at the top of the stairs was Richard's bedroom.

He'd been stupid to say to Adam Meade that he was Richard's boyfriend. It wasn't really like that. He and Richard had gone to bed together a number of times but they both knew, he suspected, that this wasn't going to turn into a long-term relationship. Boyfriend was a term that gave the wrong impression.

It was the swimming pool that had brought Geoff and Richard together. They'd been at the same table at a charity auction held just before Christmas, one of those events where you pay for a mediocre meal at a hotel and then bid large sums of money for things you really don't want. Richard, he remembered, had paid £200 for a rugby ball signed by some rugby league team somewhere. He himself had made the winning £500 bid for a glass vase, made by a local craftsman glass-blower and actually a half-decent piece of work although it had remained since the auction tucked away in one of Richard's cupboards. He and Richard had started talking, and the conversation had turned to sport. Geoff had admitted to a swimming obsession and Richard told him that he had a pool ready for use. "You'd be very welcome. Really I never use it myself these days," he'd said.

So Geoff had accepted the invitation and made use of the pool on a few occasions. And then, on perhaps the fourth time, Richard had joined him in the pool. The water was warm and the weather sultry and somehow things had taken off from there. It had started, in the corny way the old song has it, with a kiss.

They had things in common. Geoff had never met Paula, Richard's ex, but he knew that the marriage had lasted more than fifteen years and the separation and divorce had been messy. He sensed that it had left Richard with an emptiness of purpose which had only partly been filled by the way he had thrown himself into his business at Greensleeves. Geoff knew the feeling. He had never anticipated finding himself single again in his forties. He and Nigel had been together for twenty years. They'd been one of the first gay couples in Lancashire to do the civil partnership thing and then, when the law changed, one of the first to go back and turn this into a marriage. Nigel's death had torn away the rock on which Geoff had built his life. One week Nigel was at the peak of fitness, charging his way round the squash court. A few weeks later he was dead of a cardiac arrest. Richard talked of his life with Paula, and in exchange listened as Geoff described his love for Nigel.

But in other ways he and Richard were poles apart, and not just when it came to interior design. Richard claimed to follow football and had a season ticket to watch Blackpool. He relished all the traditional stuff associated with being in business: the Rotary and the dinners and all that kind of thing. Geoff found that world tedious. He would have preferred a weekend at a good hotel in Oxfordshire and an evening at Garsington watching the opera to a cold Saturday afternoon on the Blackpool terraces.

They were both driven by the challenges that their businesses threw up, although Geoff privately thought he was a better businessman than Richard. There was a certain toughness, even cruelty, in the way Richard did business deals which Geoff wouldn't himself have employed. Maybe that came from Richard's childhood, growing up in a run-down estate in Morecambe. But if he was honest, Geoff thought to himself as he reached the end of the hotel's pool and flipped himself neatly round under the water to start another length, it was the toughness which Richard exuded which he also found attractive.

So had Richard fancied him? Because love wasn't the right word. They'd both, he thought, enjoyed the sex. Richard had confessed that, among all the heterosexual relationships he'd had, he'd also had a couple of gay affairs earlier in his life. So together they had settled into the sexual side of things just fine.

Geoff Handley turned at the pool end again. His pre-breakfast swim was turning into a long training session. No problem. The day could wait.

So had Richard used him? This was a much more problematic question. Had Richard effectively been after his money? Had Geoff been a convenient way of resolving some of the Greensleeves' debt issues which had been becoming an increasing cause for concern?

Oh god, that was an impossible question to answer. It was one that Geoff had been asking himself more and more in recent weeks. Maybe he had been naïve. Maybe Richard had really wanted him more for his wallet than for his body or his brain. He stopped swimming as the thought came to him and turned briefly to float on his back. Maybe he'd been taken in. Maybe he'd been conned.

Certainly Richard had not kept his side of the deal. The promised paperwork on Geoff's loan had never come through. And they had rowed about it, of course, both of them angry. They'd both made terrible threats. It was awful that the last time he'd seen Richard everything had ended as it had.

And now Richard was dead, and Geoff was left both passionately grieving a lost lover but at the same time still angry as hell.

He pulled himself from the pool, showered and went back to his room. It was only just after nine o'clock. The hotel had wifi and a comfortable lounge area and Geoff had already decided he would stay on after breakfast until lunchtime before making the journey back to the office. He needed some quiet time to assess the detailed proposals for colour schemes for the Sri Lankan contract which had come through from one of his freelance associates a few days ago and he could do that just as easily in the hotel as anywhere else. But there was another reason, too. Geoff wanted to be close to Keswick in case Adam Meade decided to get back in touch.

It was some time around mid-morning when the text he was hoping for arrived on his mobile phone. "Have been thinking about what you said," Geoff read. "Not sure, but maybe we should meet again."

Geoff immediately phoned back, but found Adam's phone ringing through to the voicemail. He texted instead: "Hi Adam. Thanks for the text. I'd really like to meet, that's fine with me. I'm flexible. Name your time and place. Geoff."

Returning to work after that was difficult. Half an hour later, and then once again around lunchtime, Geoff tried ringing Adam but still the phone went through to voicemail. Geoff deferred his departure from the hotel still later, ordering a platter of charcuterie and local cheeses and a ginger beer from the bar for his lunch. Around two o'clock he texted a second time: "Adam, hope you got my text. Have been trying to reach you all morning. When shall we meet?" Once again there was no response.

The message came through around half past three but it wasn't what he'd hoped for. A short three word text read simply 'changed my mind'.

Almost immediately the mobile rang. Geoff answered it eagerly but it was his PA ringing through, to check on his movements.

"Hi Geoff, how is it going?"

"Fine. This is a good place to get some work done," he replied.

"Good, but listen. I have two police officers who have just arrived in the office who say that they need to speak with you. They haven't told me why but it seems to be important. They're standing here in front of me now."

"Ah, OK. Want to put them on the phone?"

There was the sound of the receiver being transferred.

"Good afternoon, Mr Handley, I am sorry to disturb your working day but I am one of the officers looking into the death of Mr Richard Meade and I believe he was an acquaintance of yours. Detective Chief Inspector George Mulholland is leading the investigation and would like to talk to you. I gather you are in Keswick at present. If you leave now it will take you less than an hour to get to the police station in Whitehaven. DCI Mulholland will be waiting for you there. At four thirty."

"I'm sorry but that's not possible. I'm about to leave the Lake District to head back to my office. Whitehaven is the wrong direction."

"I do understand. Nevertheless I must insist that you change your plans a little. Let me repeat, the arrangement is for 4.30 at the Whitehaven station."

The call ended. Geoff Handley had found himself with no option but to agree.

8.

Chef was angry. The weekend was already in sight, and that meant that the number of covers they could expect in the restaurant that evening would be up on the numbers earlier in the week. He needed a full complement of staff in the kitchen.

"Where the fuck is Meade?" he expleted. "It's already nearly six o'clock. The arsehole is hours late. I'll murder him."

The other two workers in the kitchen shrugged. Chef was known for losing his rag now and again. It was best not to respond. Still, as they all knew, Adam Meade's regular shift on Thursdays was supposed to start at five. He was taking a hell of a risk showing up quite so late.

"No, take that back. I'll sack him first, and then I'll murder him," Chef continued. He turned to one of his staff. "Go up to his room and find him. Bring him down here in the next five minutes in his fucking pyjamas if you have to."

"Yes, Chef." The man left promptly. Chef glared round at the one staff member he had left.

"All right, get the asparagus prepared. I want them looking like a nice pert row of erect penises. Don't stare at me like that, get working."

Silence descended on the kitchen. Chef took himself off to do something to the venison medallions.

The kitchen door re-opened almost immediately.

"He's not there. Adam's not in his room," came the report. "And all his stuff's gone too. I'll don't know, Chef, but it looks like he may have decided to leave."

"Fucking hell. I should have got rid of him days ago. He's been a pain all week."

The two other members of staff exchanged glances. With Meade not there, the evening was going to be very long and very fraught.

Chef pulled out his mobile phone and began typing a text, saying the words aloud with emphasis as he did. "Dear Mr Fucking Meade," he started. "I have no fucking idea why you are not at work but whatever your excuse take it from me that you are herewith sacked. Don't ever dare to return to my kitchen. PS I hope you never find work in a kitchen again."

He pushed the send button with a flourish.

"Stop fannying about, start working," he said to his remaining staff.

9.

Jack Higgins let himself in to his bungalow, took off his coat and made for the fridge. He pulled out one of the cans of John Smith's from the large cardboard box they were packed in at the supermarket and which he'd put straight in the fridge to chill, box unopened. He drank the beer down hurriedly and reached for a second can.

His life was falling to pieces again and he had no-one any more to talk to him, to get him back to rights. And to tell him off for drinking too much, as he knew he was. The bottle of whisky he'd bought last week was already much emptier than it should have been. Oh god, things were getting him down at the moment. He was very hard up. But, more than anything else, he was lonely as hell.

The day had been one with just the usual standard degree of horribleness until the afternoon, when the two policewomen had shown up. All his adult life he'd kept away from the police as much as he could. He'd had too many dealings with the police when he was younger, and he knew that somewhere on some police file or other his name was still there, waiting to be dug out once again. The two police officers who'd interviewed him wouldn't even have been born when all that business happened but no doubt they'd already checked him out. John Murray Higgins, they'd have known all about him.

He hated the way the police these days pretended to be all friendly and understanding. "So sorry to take so much of your time, Mr Higgins," the slightly older woman had said to him when she'd started off her questioning. He'd have preferred her to have dropped the pretence. "All right, Higgins, tell us the fucking truth. You wanted your boss dead, didn't you?" That's what he'd rather she'd have said. Because, after half an hour of weasel words that was basically what she'd asked him anyway, although not in quite that language of course. And effectively he'd answered yes.

The two young women in their neat little police uniforms played the game differently from the old days, but underneath it was the same old game. Cat and mouse. The cats are polite and call you 'Mister' and offer you a glass of water and all that, but they are still cats. And you are still the mouse, for them to play with.

So after endless preliminaries, the interview had moved on to talk about his relationship with Meade. They'd asked him all about the business relationship. Yes, he'd told them, he and Meade had bought Greensleeves together. Yes, 2002, it was. Yes, from old Terry Donnelly, who was well past retirement and quite rightly wanted to get his money out and enjoy himself.

More questions. Yes, he'd already been working at Greensleeves, basically as Donnelly's right-hand man. Yes, he knew the business, and knew it could be made to work. Yes, he'd saved some money over the years. No, it wasn't enough. He had enough to meet about half the asking price, that was all. So, yes, he'd gone into partnership with Meade. Worst decision of his life, he told them. That had made them sit up.

How had he known Meade? He'd bought a couple of motors from him. The cars had been a fair price and hadn't broken down, so that seemed a good omen. He and Meade both had season tickets for Blackpool, too. It's a small club, and they'd sometimes met up on match days. And Higgins thought they had complementary things to contribute to Greensleeves. He had the inside knowledge of how the park functioned day to day. Meade had more business experience than he did. A marriage made in heaven.

Except, as he told the police, it was actually a marriage made in hell. No point in beating about the bush. All the other staff at Greensleeves knew the story anyway and knew what he thought of Meade and they'd certainly be ready to spill the beans to the coppers if they hadn't already done so. Might as well tell it like it was.

So, next set of questions, what had happened next? Yes, Meade had bought him out. 2006. Why? Because he desperately needed the money. Higgins didn't want to say why – it was, after all, a personal matter – but the bastard police had insisted. In the end he told them the full story. They'd been irritatingly understanding.

Had it been a fair price?, they'd asked him. Of course it hadn't been a fair price, he'd answered. Meade had had him. Meade had tied him to the floor and jumped up and down on his balls. Metaphorically speaking, of course.

And the worst thing was, when all the legal stuff had been agreed and signed and the money paid by Meade to him (and almost as soon spent), that he'd had to go on working at Greensleeves. As Meade's minion. His role was there just to be made to cut the grass and to stick his arm up to his elbow in the drains trying to unblock the sewage system which as everyone knew very well was fucked.

So when the policewoman who was leading the interview had asked him what he'd thought of Meade after all this had happened, he'd been ready with the answer. "I hated him," Higgins had told her. "And you can put that in your report that you're going to write when you finally let me get home. Talking of which, I want to get home as soon as possible. So could you please hurry up with any other questions you want me to answer?"

At which point the two policewomen had just smiled beatifically at him and the one in charge had said something to him like, "I can assure you, Mr Higgins, that we won't keep you here a moment longer than is necessary." And then they had started all over again with a whole set of other questions.

Did he drive? Did he know the Lake District? Why hadn't he done the Three Peaks with all the rest of the staff?

And in particular: What was he doing last Saturday evening? That was the question they were really interested in, Higgins could tell.

"I was at home," he'd told them.

And was there anyone else who could vouch for that?

"No, of course not, I was at home alone."

Still more questions. Eventually Higgins had been able to stand it no more.

"Look, I've told you there was no love lost between Meade and me. I won't pretend I'm mourning his death and I assure you I won't be the only one who feels the same way. But why would I want to waste the small amount of my own spare time to go to the Lake District to bump him off? Haven't you looked in my store at Greensleeves? Don't you know the stocks of chemicals I've got there? If I'd wanted to, I could have finished off Meade any time I chose."

"I see, Mr Higgins," the policewoman had said at this point. "Thank you for being so frank with us."

Looking back on the way the interview had gone, Higgins thought perhaps that he should have refused to let the police get under his skin quite so much. He should have played their game back to them, all cool and polite. But that just wasn't his way. Perhaps he'd told them more than he should have. Tough, too late now.

Jack Higgins went across and put the television on. It was much later than he normally would have got home from work, the news and regional news programmes were long over. Still, that meant that the rest of the evening wouldn't drag on so long. He went back to the fridge and reached for a third beer.

10.

For Nick Potterton, the evening was promising to be altogether a lot more enjoyable than the night before in the Traveller's Rest. He was in the bar of the Black Bull in Coniston, sharing a drink with several members of his running club. Thursday evening was the time for the regular weekly pack run for the Coniston and Hawkshead Harriers, and after an hour and a half spent running over the nearby Coniston fells most of the runners gathered together in the pub to socialise.

Given the day he'd had, Nick had nearly decided not to go to the pack run. But, as so often when he made the effort, he had enjoyed the satisfaction that had come from some hard physical exercise. They'd initially started from Coniston village south-westwards, running on tracks and sheep paths which skirted the great hulk of Coniston Old Man. They'd stopped briefly at the little mountain tarn known as Goat's Water and then tackled the stiff climb up on to the plateau and on to the summit of the Old Man itself. The pack run had ended with a fast descent back down to Coniston village, nestling two thousand feet or so below.

It had been wonderful summer weather and they'd watched the sun drop down over the distant Irish Sea in a glorious glow of evening sunlight. What a beautiful place the Lake District was, Nick thought. How lucky he was to live where he did.

Lindsay Maddens, still in her running kit, came across the pub to join him at the table where he was sitting. It was the first time they'd seen each other since their day together spent combing the flanks of Lingmell with the mountain rescue team on Sunday afternoon.

"Hi Lindsay," Nick said. "I was thinking, how do you fancy a meal at my place on Saturday night? You and Phil of course. Seven-ish?"

"Love to. By the way, is everything all right, Nick? I heard some gossip about you from some of the others in mountain rescue," Lindsay began.

Nick dropped his voice, to avoid being overheard. "I don't know what you heard, but it's probably true." He briefly described the conversation he had had with Pat that morning.

"That's pretty harsh," Lindsay replied. "Do you think the police asked Pat to ban you?"

"Perhaps. It's true that I'm not the police's favourite journalist just at the moment."

"I read the *Enquirer* this morning," Lindsay went on.

"Yes. What do you think?" Nick asked.

Lindsay paused before replying.

"Well, I suppose I must admit that I'm not completely convinced by the story."

"You mean, the front page lead."

"Yes. I still think it could have been natural... the death I mean. We know what a shitty night it was early on Sunday morning. A short time on the hills without the right gear and hypothermia would get you."

"I know," Nick replied. "But the body was found with most of the clothes removed. That's pretty curious, you have to accept."

"Yes I read that bit of the article too," Lindsay said. "But..."

Nick looked at her. "But what?"

"Well, I remembered one of our mountain rescue training sessions on hypothermia. You must remember it."

"Which one?"

"The one led by the guy from A&E at West Cumberland Hospital. The session that mentioned paradoxical undressing."

"Sorry, Lindsay, what did you just say?"

"Paradoxical undressing. You recall, it's what medics use to describe what happens when hypothermia victims do the opposite of what seems logical, and actually start removing their own clothes. Their bodies are telling them that they're too hot, not too cold. It's a fairly well-known syndrome. Taking off their clothes can be almost the last thing somebody does when they're suffering from exposure before they lie down and die."

"Yes, I do remember now that we covered that in the training. I'd forgotten."

Nick thought this through, and went on. "So, let me get this straight. What you're suggesting is that if this were a case of paradoxical undressing, Richard Meade would have taken off his clothes himself."

"That's what I'm saying."

"Richard Meade would have undressed himself."

"Yes, he would have done."

"And nobody else would necessarily have been around."

"No."

Another pause.

"So the implication would be... that his death wasn't murder at all," Nick continued.

"Not murder at all," Lindsay Maddens echoed.

"Just natural causes," Nick went on. "And our front page would be entirely misleading."

"Well, yes, it would," Lindsay replied.

"Shit."

"Not a case of murder, just a case of very bad luck in very bad weather."

Friday

1.

Jemima Goodchild took a little more care than usual over her clothes and make-up and brushed her blonde hair carefully. Of course, if you worked in a solicitors' office you needed to dress smartly: the public expected it, and first impressions were important.

There was another reason. Today was Friday and today at 9am one of her firm's new clients was due to come in for his appointment. He'd called in on Wednesday morning, and although they'd only exchanged a few words at the time as she made the booking for him she'd liked what she'd seen. And he'd smiled at her, in a particular sort of way. He was good-looking and just at the moment she was single. Oh well, worth taking a little trouble getting ready. You never knew when fortune would smile on you.

Jemima arrived at the reception desk in good time to open up, at 8.45am. The minutes slipped by: there were various telephone calls to answer and pass through to the firm's solicitors and legal clerks and there were a couple of callers who came in to make or change an appointment. But nobody else arrived.

At 9.15am an internal telephone call came through from the upstairs extension where one of the firm's partners, a solicitor by the name of Jane Evans, had her desk.

"Hi Jemima, what's happened to my Nine O'Clock?" she asked. "Didn't you book me in a new client?"

"Yes, I did, but he's not shown up."

"Oh well, I've got plenty of paperwork to catch up with. In the scheme of things I suppose it doesn't really matter."

"No, I suppose it doesn't," Jemima replied, with a sigh.

2.

Nick and Molly were in Molly's office, each drinking a mug of instant coffee. An unpleasant smell of eucalyptus from Molly's vaping habit permeated the place. Still, Nick thought, it was better than the atmosphere Molly had previously worked in when she had chain-smoked her way through the working day.

"You're telling me we may not have a story any more?" Molly asked incredulously.

"I'm telling you that our headline next week could be "The Body in the Bog – Actually It Wasn't Murder". I think you'll agree it's not the most dramatic front page splash that the *Enquirer*'s ever had."

Molly grimaced. "You'd better tell me what you've found out."

Nick had gone online as soon as he had returned the evening before from Coniston, and sure enough Google had supplied him with links to some heavyweight medical studies on hypothermia. He called these up now on Molly's monitor and together they looked at them. There could be no doubt about it. It was possible that Meade, in an advanced stage of hypothermia, had taken off his clothes himself.

"I offered to buy George Mulholland a drink if I beat him to the solution of the Meade business. Looks like I'll be buying the round. Although..." Molly tailed off.

"I know," Nick responded. "It still doesn't hang together. The business of Meade pretending to be on the phone in the middle of the night in Wasdale. The call yesterday from his son, saying that his father had felt at risk. And that he himself was frightened."

"What's happened about Adam Meade?"

"That's a problem. I tried to ring him late last night and again before I came to work today but he didn't answer. I think the phone's switched off. '"

"We don't know where he's living?"

"No, only that he's somewhere in Cumbria. I've got his mother's address though," Nick said.

Molly mulled this over.

"I think we give this story our best efforts for one more day. If we don't get much further by this evening we'll agree to put a small downpage piece on one of the inside news pages next week. And then we'll have to get a new front page lead from somewhere."

Nick nodded in agreement. "How shall we split the work? I'd planned to try to talk to the handyman at Greensleeves today, if you still want me to go."

"Why don't you do that? Follow up Meade's business dealings? I know you love all that sort of stuff. I'll see if I can get anywhere with Adam Meade's mother. Let me have her details. And now tell me about your burglary."

Nick gave Molly a very brief account of what had happened.

"'Shadowy Intruder puts Frighteners on Nuclear Power Researcher'. That could be the replacement front page story we need," she responded.

"Don't you dare," Nick replied. "Anyway I've no proof. As far as I can tell the text of my book's not been tampered with. I phoned the union for legal advice and they told me to take sensible precautions and keep a backup of the text somewhere else. I had already. In fact, I've got the memory stick in my pocket. I mean, we all know that if you do investigative work other parties can sometimes begin to take an interest in what you're finding out."

"I suppose so. The *Cumbrian Enquirer* has only been burgled once and curiously that wasn't to check up on a story we were running, it was to nick our SLR cameras. The police never caught anyone."

"Talking of the police, are you going to say anything to George Mulholland?"

"Yes, I think I'll give him a ring. Crow a little that we've cracked the mystery, even if we haven't quite yet. I'll ring him over lunch, when he's most likely to be out of meetings."

"All right, I'll make my way down to Greensleeves. Maybe catch up with you at lunchtime?"

"Good idea."

3.

George Mulholland had assembled the team for what was becoming the regular morning meeting.

"Good morning again ladies and gentlemen," he began. "Thank you for all your efforts yesterday afternoon. We are moving forward, I think. There has, however, been a less welcome development. Sergeant Nickleby will tell us about that in a moment, won't you Patrick?"

The plain-clothes officer nodded.

"First, we have the transcripts of the interviews with Mr Geoffrey Handley, the business acquaintance and friend of Meade, of Mr Jack Higgins and of Ms Monica Roughlee, both employees of Meade at his Greensleeves park. As you know, I interviewed Handley here. He's a bright cookie. I formally cautioned him five minutes into the interview. It had the desired effect, took the wind out of his sails. And of course it means the interview can be used as evidence. No charges yet." The room nodded its understanding.

"Two salient things. Handley admitted that he had given Meade £60,000 a few weeks back. He was unable to say, however, whether this was a loan and if so what the terms were. He said that he and Meade had still not finalised the agreement. There was clearly an issue between them here. You could tell from Handley's body language. He also admitted after questioning that he and Meade had had sexual intercourse on several occasions in recent weeks.

"The second thing relates to Handley's movements last weekend. He has no alibi to offer for Saturday night. He told me he was in his flat in Lancaster. He said he was spending the evening in alone with Rigoletto."

Mulholland paused. There were a few blank looks around the room.

"A classical opera by Verdi, for those among us who prefer Radio 2. Handley has good musical taste – if of course he really was listening to a CD in his flat as he says, and not secretly listening to Radio 2 as he drove through the Cumbrian lanes to Wasdale that evening. At the moment, we can't be sure. We are in the process of checking numberplate IDs from the M6 although he could have deliberately chosen to avoid the motorway. I have impounded his Lexus so we can do forensic work on it, although it looks unfortunately rather clean. I've also temporarily taken custody of his laptop. Handley is not best pleased. He has stayed in Whitehaven overnight, so on the bright side that's a boost for our poor depressed local economy. I told him to return at eleven and I'm sure he will. Now, then, Sergeant Chambers. Tell us about your afternoon."

"Thank you sir. As DCI Mulholland has said the interviews have been transcribed and are on the system. Monica Roughlee is a young woman employee who told us originally that Meade was using his mobile phone at Wasdale Head, but it turns out she was several rows back in the minibus and not in a position to hear anything or know for sure. I heard all about her problems with her walking boots but very little that is pertinent to the enquiry. I don't think Roughlee needs to be of much further interest to us. Jack Higgins is a different matter. He is the maintenance worker at the Greensleeves park. He confirmed what Malcolm Macdonald told us yesterday. He was originally Meade's business partner. They bought the park together in 2002 and Meade bought him out in 2006.

"Higgins was pretty forthright in his views on Meade in the interview. He obviously still felt bitter that he'd had to sell his share of the business. It was clear that there was no love lost between him and Meade. He'd stayed on as an employee, but you felt Greensleeves was the last place he really wanted to be working."

Chrissy Chambers paused. She realised she had the room's attention.

"After I had pushed him, Higgins told me that he had sold up to Meade because he urgently needed the money to pay care fees for his wife. His wife, he said, had been diagnosed with an incurable degenerative condition and at that time needed pretty well constant nursing. She died in 2007, he said. We can check this out, but it sounds genuine. It's not the sort of thing you'd invent.

"There are a couple of other things. Higgins struck me as prone to temper. We've checked of course and he had a conviction for taking part in a street brawl when he was much younger. The original charge was GBH, but he pleaded guilty to breach of the peace and the GBH case was never heard in court. He was bound over. Since then his record has been clean.

"But he has no alibi for Saturday night. He says he has lived alone since his wife died. What he told me was that he stayed up last Saturday watching television until Match of the Day had ended and then he went to bed. He also suggested in as many words that, had he been so minded, he could have finished off Meade without needing to go to the Lakes to do it. So not precisely playing the old nicey-nicey middle-class card to us."

George Mulholland intervened. "Does he drive?"

"Yes, sir, he drives but he told us that he hasn't got a car at the moment and the DVLA database confirms that. So if he was involved in the weekend's events, he would either have needed an accomplice or had to hire a car. I've arranged for local car hire firms to be spoken to, but nothing has come back yet. And, besides, Higgins may be plain-speaking but he's not stupid. If he needed a car last Saturday but didn't want us to know, he wouldn't have hired it locally. We've not had a chance yet to check more widely."

"Thank you, Chrissy. So, apart from all that, what do you *think*?" George Mulholland was looking straight at her.

"My instinct, you mean? I think it's most likely he was indeed watching Match of the Day. But – well, I've learned since I joined the force that we need to be guided above all by the evidence."

"Yes, we do," Mulholland replied. Chrissy Chambers felt almost as if she was being quizzed by him for a job interview. She felt she'd done all right.

"And now then, Patrick," Mulholland went on. "I asked you yesterday to interview Meade's son Adam. Your news is troubling. Tell us."

"Yes, sir. We tracked down that Adam Meade was working as a junior chef in the kitchen of a hotel in Keswick, and I went there with DC Probert yesterday afternoon. We arrived there at about 4.15pm and spoke to the hotel manager. He took us up to the room where Adam Meade was being billeted. Meade had worked the lunchtime shift and was due back in the kitchen at 5pm, so this was supposed to be his afternoon break. The room was empty, and I mean completely empty. Meade had obviously packed his bags some time shortly after lunch and left. We interviewed the manager, who said that he had seen and heard nothing. Meade had not given in his notice."

Mulholland took over. "So we now have a dead person called Richard Meade and a missing person, his son. Let me remind you that Adam Meade was also a director of Greensleeves, albeit an inactive one. I have already circulated his details to other forces. I arranged yesterday for Humberside police to contact his mother and brother as a matter of urgency, to see what they say. And to get a recent photo of him. I will also brief the media this afternoon. We need to find Adam Meade urgently, to eliminate him as a possible suspect of course but also to ensure he is safe. Greensleeves has already lost one of its directors and I don't want to lose a second one. That's it for now. The investigation will continue over the weekend so you know what to do. Cancel any weddings you may have arranged with your fiancées for tomorrow. We'll reconvene here first thing tomorrow."

The room emptied. George Mulholland reached for his phone, picked up the receiver and phoned a mobile phone number.

"Molly, it's George," he said.

"Hello, George. Funnily enough I was about to ring you."

"I thought you deserved to know first. I'm calling another press briefing this afternoon. Richard Meade's son Adam has disappeared from where he was living in Keswick and we are at the moment having to treat him as a missing person. Of course there may be a simple explanation to his disappearance but just as a precaution we will be releasing his details to the media and asking the public to look out for him. You may be able to help us too."

"I see, George," Molly replied. "What I need to tell you in exchange is that Adam Meade rang us yesterday. He claimed that his father had been worried about his safety before last weekend's development. Adam added that he was worried about his own safety. Adam was speaking to one of my reporters."

There was an intake of breath at the other end of the phone. "Not to Mr Potterton by any chance?"

"Yes, to Nick."

"Molly, this was information which should have been immediately communicated to the police. Why did Mr Potterton disregard the law? This is serious."

"George, please. Nick and I agreed this morning that I would ring you and brief you. And indeed to share with you something else which we've discovered and which is highly relevant. Do you know how to use Google?"

"Molly, don't patronise me. I'm feeling quite annoyed with you already. I could send officers to arrest you both for obstructing my enquiry."

"Come and arrest me, you'd be doing me a favour. I need a good strong story for my page one lead," Molly replied. "Although before you instruct the uniformed branch to clap me in irons, you might want to do the Google search first. There are two words you need to put into the search engine."

George repeated back what Molly told him.

"All right, I'll do what you suggest," he said. He paused and then went on. "You know, we always used to work well together. I don't want us to fall out over this."

"I don't want to either, George. I appreciate you calling me. Keep in touch."

4.

Even with the address, it hadn't been easy for Molly to get in touch with Adam's mother. Eventually via the electoral roll Molly found out the current surname Paula was using and that, together with the BT online directory, delivered the phone number. As Molly had feared, there was no answer when she rang. But she was in luck: the voicemail message from Paula Pettifer provided her with Paula's mobile number.

Molly found herself talking to a very distracted woman.

"Sorry, who did you say you were?" Paula mumbled.

Molly introduced herself a second time.

"Oh, I thought you were perhaps from the police. They've been round, you know. They've told me Adam's disappeared. I'm so worried about him."

"I'm sure you are," Molly responded. "Have you any idea where he might be?"

"No, the police asked me that too. I rang the hotel where he was working but they said they didn't know anything. They weren't very friendly towards me. They said that Adam just packed his things and went yesterday afternoon."

"Did Adam have any friends he might be visiting?"

"He'd have told me. His mobile's gone dead. I can't understand it."

"Was Adam very upset about his father's death?"

"Well, yes, I'm sure he was. Adam's still only a young lad. You know he came with me to... to identify the body?"

Molly's pencil made Teeline shapes.

"No, I don't think I knew that."

"Adam was in a strange mood that morning. But I can't say I was much better. It's horrible, I don't want to think about it. I wouldn't wish that experience on my worst enemy."

"I understand," Molly paused. "Have you been in touch with Adam since he left you on Tuesday?"

"No. Although I saw I'd had a missed call from him yesterday. But he'd have left a message if it had been important."

Molly wondered how far she could push the conversation. At the other end of the phone was clearly a woman in some distress. Molly decided to carry on as long as she could.

"Paula, forgive me for asking you this but you know that Adam's father's death is still unexplained and there is a suggestion of foul play. Have you any thoughts on how your former husband might have died?"

"No. I mean Richard wasn't stupid. He was somebody who was always in control of things. Maybe it was an accident. I can't believe he'd take his own life."

"Did he have enemies? I mean, perhaps business people he owed money to?"

"I suppose it's possible. Adam told me on Tuesday that Greensleeves was struggling financially. But Richard said exactly the same thing to me when we got divorced, just so I wouldn't ask him for any more money in the settlement."

"Were you and Richard together a long time?"

"Fifteen years."

"The separation must have been painful."

"Yes, it was. But it was the right decision.

"Was he – please excuse me for asking you this so bluntly – was he unfaithful?"

"Yes, of course he was unfaithful. I knew about the affairs. Well, most of them I knew about. But that wasn't the thing really."

"No?" Molly prompted her.

"He loved having power. He never abused me physically. I wouldn't have stood for it for a moment. But he abused me in another way. He made me feel worthless and small and irrelevant. That's terribly undermining, you know. In the end I think I only just got out in time."

"So what about Adam himself? Could he have got on the wrong side of anyone?"

"No, oh please god no. No, surely he'd have told me if he was in trouble."

The woman Molly was speaking to was becoming more and more distraught. Human decency meant that the telephone call had to end, whatever the journalistic needs of the *Enquirer*.

"All right, Paula, I'm sorry to have disturbed you," Molly said.

"Please help me. I'm so frightened that something terrible has happened to Adam. Can you ask your readers to look out for him?"

"We'll try to help. And I'm sure Adam will be in touch with you again very soon."

Molly terminated the call. Was she sure Adam would be in touch soon? Actually she wasn't sure at all.

5.

"She's at home with a migraine. Well, actually she's worried she has septicaemia. From the blisters, you know."

The speaker was Peggy in the Greensleeves office, and she was talking to Nick Potterton. His third visit to Greensleeves in five days was not off to the best of starts.

"We're not sure why, but the police interviewed her again last night. Just her and Jack Higgins. Two women police officers. I think that was the last straw for her," Peggy went on.

"Not to worry," Nick responded. "Tell Monica when you see her to look after herself. I'll just see if Jack Higgins is here before I leave."

Jack Higgins was in his store-room, tinkering with the mowing machine. He looked up as Nick pushed open the door.

"I know you didn't want to talk to me on Monday but I wonder if you'll spare me five minutes now," Nick began.

There was a noncommittal response from Jack Higgins.

"My newspaper reported Richard Meade's death in this week's edition. This will mean big changes at Greensleeves. I... I wanted to ask your opinion on what will happen. I know you used to co-own the business with him."

Jack Higgins took time before replying. "First it was the bloody police and now it's the bloody press. But since you're here you'd better sit down." He pointed to an old metal chair at the back of the room, which Nick dragged forward. Higgins himself perched on a stool beside the work-bench."

"It was a wrench selling your share of Greensleeves, I think," Nick said. It was a guess, but a good one.

There was another long pause but eventually Jack Higgins began talking. He described how he and Richard Meade had taken the decision to buy Greensleeves together and then how Meade had bought him out.

"I told the policewomen all this yesterday evening, so I might as well tell you too." he said. "I'll be honest. By the end I hated Meade."

"I understand," Nick replied. "Didn't he recently ask you though to buy back in?"

"He had this mad idea to sell the staff shares in Greensleeves from their wages. I told him he had a fucking nerve to ask me."

"Of course. He was in debt, I think."

"The mortgage company are clamouring for cash. He'd just about run out of ideas for what to do."

"There was a new shareholder called Geoff, wasn't there?"

"Was there? News to me. Stupid man."

"What about Richard Meade's sons? What about Adam?"

"Adam was a mushroom. Kept in the dark and fed you-know-what. Adam will probably find himself having to pick up the pieces and paying all the debts. Good luck to him."

"Have you met him?"

"I knew Adam and Dan when they were kids. Before Meade's divorce. And Meade brought Adam down here a couple of times more recently. Nice kid."

"How did you get out of the Three Peaks trip?"

"I don't do mountains. And maybe I shouldn't say this but I was afraid Meade might be tempted to keep the sponsorship money to help the business. He would have told himself that it was just a temporary thing, just for a week or two before he passed the money to the hospice. Maybe I'm maligning him."

"Will Greensleeves pull through, do you think?"

"What gets me so angry is that Greensleeves could be a good little business if it was properly managed. Meade and I drew a decent return when we ran it together. And we treated the residents fairly in those days, too. Played by the book."

"Not tempted to give it another go?"

"Too old."

Nick nodded, and changed the subject.

"How did Meade die, do you think?"

"No idea, but not suicide. Meade wasn't that kind. He was too full of his next great plan," Jack Higgins replied. "And just before you ask, no, I didn't murder him. The police asked me that, I mean not directly, but that was clearly what they were getting at. And I can see that you're wondering too. A convenient Cluedo solution: it was Mr Higgins on the mountain-side with a lump of lead piping. But no, it wasn't, not this time."

Nick laughed. It was true that Higgins had indeed given an answer to the one question which had been very much in Nick's mind over the past few minutes. Slightly taken aback, Nick decided to play along with Higgins' direct approach. "So you obviously have a cast-iron alibi for last Saturday night. You were with Colonel Mustard in the billiard room," he said.

"An alibi? Of course I don't have an alibi. I was alone at home."

Jack Higgins paused momentarily. "Ellen and I used to go out at weekends, but let me tell you, you no longer fancy it when you find yourself living alone."

"I think I know what you mean," Nick said. He knew very well.

6.

"Bingo!"

Detective sergeant Kate Morgan, George Mulholland's office manager for the enquiry, came through the door of his office beaming.

"Mr Handley's car numberplate has shown up. His car was being driven north on the M6 north of Lancaster at 7.21pm last Saturday evening."

Mulholland immediately looked up from his desk.

"Early on Saturday evening. I see."

"So Handley was not in his Lancaster flat that evening. Unless of course someone else was the driver of his vehicle," Kate Morgan continued.

"What about southbound records? When did he travel back? Saturday night? Sunday morning? Some other time?"

"This is not quite so straightforward. The data from last weekend seems to be corrupted. I've got someone urgently on the case."

"Mr Handley is due here in half an hour. I think he hopes I will give him back his laptop and his car. Make sure there's an interview room available for me for when he arrives."

"I will." Kate Morgan left the office.

7.

"Adam's disappeared. George rang me shortly after you left. The police are going public shortly."

Molly was in her office. Nick had just arrived back from his visit to Greensleeves.

"Disappeared?"

"That's what George said. The Humberside police have been round to see his mother, too."

"Bloody hell. What do you think?"

"Not sure. You'd almost convinced me that Meade died of natural causes. A simple case of someone caught out on the fells in bad weather and ending up in Dickie's Meadow."

"Ending up where?"

"In Dickie's Meadow. Don't you know the saying?"

"No, I don't think so. Where's Dickie's Meadow?"

"Maybe it's something we say just in this part of England. It's another way of saying that you're up a creek where you'd rather not be without a paddle. Or in fact, where you'd rather not be even if you did have a paddle."

"Got you."

"Richard Meade in Dickie's Meadow. It's appropriate."

Nick gave a weak smile. "So where now with our story for next week's paper?" he went on. "By the way, will there even *be* a paper next week?"

"The *Enquirer*'s financial problems? We've got a few more months at least. I'm seeing this business advisor next Wednesday. I might come back to you about the crowdfunding idea after that."

"OK, let me know."

"Did you glean anything new at Greensleeves?"

"Not much. Higgins, Meade's old business partner, thought Meade might have planned to pocket the sponsorship money himself. But I called through to the hospice manager on my mobile while I was still down there. Meade had already paid across the money he'd raised himself. Several thousand, I gather. Even before he'd set off for the Three Peaks."

"Did that mean he knew in advance that he wouldn't be completing the challenge?"

"Maybe. The hospice sang his praises to high heaven, by the way. He could do no wrong in their eyes."

"A good man fallen among thieves, perhaps."

"Sorry to correct you Molly but I think the Bible says it was a poor man who fell among thieves. Which might be true too. I don't think Meade had much money to call his own at the end."

8.

George Mulholland was prepared to be patient. He had arrested Handley when the man had returned to Whitehaven police station that morning. Mulholland's opinion was that Handley could potentially be charged with perverting the course of justice but failing that there was always the useful catch-all of wasting police time. And who knew, later on there might be rather more serious charges.

Handley had insisted on his rights and had put a call through to the solicitor he used for his business affairs. She was in Lancaster, but had promised to set off immediately. That would mean a wait of about two hours or so.

Mulholland smiled encouragingly. "That's fine, Mr Handley. Sergeant Chambers here will arrange for you to be taken down to the cells. I'm afraid we will have to ask you to empty all your pockets. And remove your belt."

Chrissy Chambers took Handley from the room.

A spell in the cells wasn't a bad thing. It could encourage Handley to be rather more cooperative later on. Mulholland turned back to his papers.

The police media team had already started putting things in place for the briefing he would be giving that afternoon. Humberside police had tracked down Adam's mother and had been given a set of photos which could be released to the media. Mulholland looked at them: he saw a young man, smiling broadly, probably taken on holiday or at a party. Adam had been rather more careworn when Mulholland had met him on Tuesday morning.

He turned to the sheaf of papers which Kate Morgan had printed off the internet for him, after he had come off the phone to Molly at the *Enquirer*. It had to be said that the material was compelling. Paradoxical undressing! Who knew there was such a syndrome? Mulholland mulled it over. Yes, he was prepared to accept that this could explain Meade's lack of clothing. But it didn't explain why Meade had left the safety of the minibus, he reminded himself.

"Kate," he called through to the neighbouring office. "I'd like to have another look at Mr Meade's mobile phone records. The ones Chrissy Chambers got from the network company on Monday. They're on the enquiry database, I assume?"

"Yes, sir."

"All right, I'd like to be undisturbed for half an hour. Fend off anyone who wants me."

9.

"I'm afraid I didn't tell you the whole truth yesterday," Geoff Handley had begun when finally he and his solicitor had been escorted to the interview room.

"No, Mr Handley, you didn't. I'm tired of your tall tales about Rigoletto. Suppose this time you explain exactly what you were doing when you drove up the M6 on Saturday evening?"

Geoff Handley paled.

"Ah, yes. I should have told you. It was a stupid idea, but I had hoped I would see Adam Meade. I felt I could save him from making a bad mistake. And his dad too."

"You planned to see Mr Adam Meade. Where?"

"Richard had let slip to me that Adam had got a job in Keswick. He'd mentioned the name of the hotel. So I decided to drive there, to try to see him."

"Did you tell anyone? Did Mr Meade senior know?"

"No, and I couldn't find Adam's phone number. Richard had given it to me, but the note where I'd written it down had got filed by mistake with some business papers. It turned up a day too late."

"So you drove to Keswick on the off-chance?"

"Yes, it was in hindsight a really crazy thing to do, but I was trying to be helpful."

"Did you see Mr Adam Meade?"

"No, that was the worst of it. When I got to the hotel, it became obvious that Adam was at work, in the kitchen. I sat down in the restaurant and ordered a meal. I thought maybe Adam would come out at some stage and I'd be able to talk to him.

"The meal was pretty mediocre but I said afterwards it was delicious and I'd like to compliment the chefs. But all that happened was that the head Chef came out to my table, a big burly guy. I could see someone who I thought was Adam behind the swing door but I couldn't think of a way to communicate with him."

"At what time approximately did you finish your meal, Mr Handley?"

"About half past nine, I suppose. The restaurant was just beginning to empty. I ordered a coffee and drank it as slowly as I could. And then..."

"Go on," Mulholland ordered.

"Then I lost my nerve, I suppose. The whole thing seemed quite ridiculous. I went back to my car and drove home to Lancaster."

Mulholland allowed a long pause to develop.

"Think very carefully, Mr Handley. Are you sure you drove from Keswick to Lancaster? Let me put it to you that you did not drive home at this point. Let me suggest that you drove westwards, until you were in the valley of Wasdale. Where you would later meet up with your lover Mr Richard Meade."

"No!" Geoff Handley almost shouted. "That's absolutely not what happened. I drove from Keswick straight home. And then I listened to music. It was true what I told you, I put Verdi on the CD machine."

"You drove up the M6 from Lancaster to Keswick, you had a meal, you did not speak to anyone apart from the head Chef and presumably the waiter, and you went straight home. Is that correct?"

"Yes."

"Yesterday you told me lies, Mr Handley. Let me ask you again. Is this the truth?"

"Absolutely."

"Why were you keen to see Mr Adam Meade? What was the bad mistake, as you called it, that you wanted him not to make."

"I thought Richard was planning to call on Adam that evening in the hotel. I thought he had arranged for the minibus to call in there. It seemed to explain everything. The excuse would have been that people needed to have a proper evening meal before carrying on up the next of the Three Peaks. And that would have given Richard the chance to talk to Adam."

"About what?"

"Richard needed Adam to agree to a deal. He needed Adam's signature on a loan form. I thought it would be a disaster."

"Mr Handley, you told us yesterday you had given £60,000 to Mr Richard Meade, but you were unable to say on what terms. Are you now saying that Mr Meade was seeking a further loan?"

"Yes, Richard was desperate. He was trying to borrow another £30,000 for the business. It wasn't from a registered credit provider, it was just from a guy Richard knew who did money-lending. The interest charged would have been horrendous. It would have been the end of the business."

"What about your money?"

"Yes, now you mention it I was worried about that, too. Obviously I would have lost it. Richard and I still hadn't agreed anything in writing. I thought I'd find Richard as well as Adam in Keswick. As I said, it was in hindsight a crazy plan of mine. One of my worst ever."

"You expect us to believe that at this point on Saturday evening you simply gave up and went home."

"I hate to admit it but yes, I gave up." Geoff Handley was slumped in his chair. He looked done-in.

There was a knock on the door of the interview room. With considerable annoyance George Mulholland saw that Kate Morgan had put her head round the door and was signalling for his attention.

"Mr Handley, I will adjourn the interview at this point. We will recommence in five minutes. I will arrange for you and your solicitor to be offered a coffee." He announced the time for the benefit of the recording equipment and went outside into the corridor where Handley and his solicitor would not be able to hear him.

"I hope this is important, Kate."

"I think so. The M6 southbound ANPR data has come through for last weekend."

"Oh yes. And?"

"And Mr Handley's Lexus was recorded on the motorway, south of the Windermere turn on the way which leads to Lancaster. At 10.56pm. On Saturday night."

"Ah." George Mulholland exhaled slowly and re-entered the interview room.

"Well, Mr Handley, you will have longer to enjoy your coffee. I intend to adjourn this interview until later this afternoon while I follow up what you have already told me. I will arrange for you and your solicitor to have a private room. We will resume our little talk again later. I look forward to it."

Geoff Handley and his solicitor were taken from the room. Mulholland remained and signalled for Kate Morgan to join him.

"I need time to think this through. And even more urgently I have to find Adam Meade. Have our media boys and girls done their stuff?"

"Yes, the press are briefed. They're expecting a short statement from you at half past four in time for the tea-time news."

"OK. I'll make sure I'm done with Handley by then."

10.

Adam Meade made his way back slowly along the promenade in the late afternoon sunshine to the backpackers' hostel where he had booked in for a second night. It had been a frustrating day. He'd been naïve to think he'd get answers to his questions here. His dad would have laughed in his face.

He entered the hostel and crossed the cheaply furnished lounge where a television was silently playing to itself. He realised that the presenter who was speaking was one of the ITV's regional newscasters. Strange, he hadn't expected that they'd get his region's news here.

And then he froze. His own face was appearing on the screen, right in front of him. It disappeared, to be followed by a shot of the detective who had accompanied him to the morgue earlier in the week and who was saying something to the camera. A caption came up at the bottom of the screen: missing person.

He rushed from the lounge, desperate to hide his face in the privacy of the empty dormitory.

He sat on his bunk bed for more than half an hour and pondered what he could do. All his plans were unravelling. He couldn't cope any more with the way everything seemed to conspiring to get him. Now he had thrown up his job and had nowhere to live. He couldn't face the thought of what he'd do next. And he still felt very frightened.

He should ring his mother. He *would* ring his mother, but somehow he needed time. And he should ring the police, he knew that, to tell them that he wasn't a missing person at all. But the call to the police felt even more difficult to make just at the moment. He thought back to the encounter with the detective: the man seemed affable enough, but after all, he was still a policeman.

Just at this moment, he told himself, he needed someone to talk to who wasn't family and who wasn't police, but who might be interested in what he had to say. He came to a decision. He switched on his mobile phone and began texting. Eventually the message was finished and Adam pressed 'send'.

In his home in Grasmere, Nick's phone gave a small beep to advise him of a new text coming in. He finished filling the teapot and pouring himself a cup of tea before casually picking it up. Nick read the message:

"I am sorry I have not been back in touch. I would like to talk to you about my dad. I should have said all this days ago. Please come if you possibly can. Please let's meet tomorrow morning. I'm in the Isle of Man. Adam Meade"

Nick read the text twice and then phoned the number. No answer. Instead he texted back immediately: "On my way."

And only then did Nick ask himself the question he urgently needed to answer. How do you get yourself to the middle of the Irish Sea on a Friday night?

Saturday

1.

It was Saturday morning in Whitehaven police station, but for George Mulholland and his enquiry team it was another working day.

Mulholland had let Geoff Handley and the Lexus go the previous afternoon, with the proviso that there might be further questions to be answered later. He'd dealt with the media call and then slipped back to his office. He finally left for home after eight. His wife was, as always, understanding but frankly it wasn't a Friday evening to remember.

And now it was Saturday. A week since Richard Meade and his staff had set off on their Three Peaks trip. Six days since the body had been found.

Mulholland had answers to several of the problems he'd set himself back last Sunday. But the big question remained as yet unanswered.

Kate Morgan knocked on his door.

"Morning, sir."

"Morning, Kate. You know I spent time yesterday looking carefully at the mobile phone data we've got."

"Meade's phone records."

"Yes. That's it."

"Anything useful?"

"As I drove home last night a thought came to me. There was one number Meade rang regularly in the days before his death. It was to a pay-as-you-go phone which he'd taken out himself. We couldn't find out anything about it, remember?"

"Yes, I remember."

"I'm going to ring it and see who answers."

2.

Nick Potterton had driven off the ferry into a summer's day. It had been early when the boat had berthed in the Isle of Man. In fact, it had been ridiculously early. He had driven aimlessly through the centre of a deserted Douglas before eventually finding a cheap café which promised him a cooked breakfast. A copy of the *Sun* was helpfully provided on the counter to help the time pass.

He'd seen too much of the M6 the night before. After Adam Meade had texted, Nick had found that there was an evening flight out of Blackpool's little airport to the Isle of Man which left shortly before eight o'clock. Could he catch it? It would be touch-and-go. He'd thrown clothes into an overnight bag, dashed out to the car and driven down through Ambleside and Windermere towards the motorway. He'd passed the Lancaster services at twenty past six, turned off to the M55 twenty minutes later and made it into the short-stay airport car park at ten past seven. In vain. He got no further than the check-in desk.

"I'm sorry sir, the flight's full tonight. Friday evenings are always busy," the woman behind the desk had told him. "Tomorrow's early morning flight is full too, but I could probably get you on the late morning flight."

Nick had pondered his options. He was within a few miles of Greensleeves, which meant that he was close to the guest house he had stayed in on Wednesday night. Another night of B&B? The thought was profoundly depressing.

"How else can I get to the Isle of Man tonight?" he'd asked.

"I don't think you can," she'd said. "Or at least not unless you get the overnight ferry from Heysham. There's often a sailing some time in the early hours."

"Right. How do I get to Heysham?"

"You'll need to go north on the M6 and take the Lancaster turnoff."

Back at the car, Nick had reached for his phone. Adam had shown no desire to answer his mobile when Nick had tried ringing earlier but he did seem to respond to texts. Nick typed out the message: "Travelling overnight on ferry. I'm trusting you. Please don't make my journey a waste of time. Nick Potterton." Two minutes later had come the reply: "OK. Meet you clock tower Victoria Street Douglas nine am."

The breakfast whiled away an hour or so and at eight o'clock Nick strolled down towards Douglas's promenade, checking the location of the clock tower on the way. A few dog walkers and a solitary jogger were out, but otherwise the town remained deserted. Nick reached the sea and turned north. The early morning sun shone across the water but the tide was out and the beach was uninviting.

Would Adam show? Maybe, maybe not. Nick had decided at Heysham to pay the extra to bring his car across, so that at least he'd be able to see something of the island. He booked his return journey for Monday afternoon: well, why not make it a long weekend? The island had some respectable mountains and his running kit and fell shoes were in their usual place in the car boot.

He looked at his watch. 8.30am. Still half an hour to go. Journalists had to accept that sometimes their stories led nowhere. He could have fallen for one of the biggest hoaxes of his career.

3.

Adam Meade heard an unfamiliar noise from the bottom of his luggage bag as he was in the process of checking out of his hostel. It sounded like a mobile phone ringing, but it wasn't his own ring tone. His own phone was in any case switched firmly off.

He froze. Somebody was trying to reach him on his second phone, the one he never used himself. He'd forgotten he still had it with him. Maybe he should have chucked it.

The phone tinkled quietly and then quickly stopped. Adam breathed again. Obviously a wrong number. Only one other person had known about that phone, and it couldn't be them.

The phone rang a second time, and again quickly stopped. Adam pulled the phone out from the bag, and checked who had been ringing. Number withheld, he read.

The phone rang a third time, this time on and on. Adam could not bear it. He pressed the green key but said nothing.

"Hello," said a voice on the phone to the silence. "Who's that?" There was a pause. "Am I speaking to you, Adam?"

Adam paused a long time.

"Yes, it's Adam. Who are you?"

"Adam, this is George Mulholland. I'm the detective you and your mother met last Tuesday."

Adam said nothing. Eventually George Mulholland continued. "Adam, I'm going to ask you a question or two, and I want you to answer just with yes or no. Here's my first question. Are you in any physical danger?"

Adam again paused before he replied.

"No, I'm not," he said.

"Is there anyone else with you at the moment?"

"No, there isn't."

"Are you able to talk to me freely?"

"Yes."

"Adam, we have a missing person search going on for you. Your mother is very worried. Can I tell her that you're safe and OK?"

"Yes, please."

"I need to talk to you about your dad. Can you help me understand how he may have died?"

Mulholland heard silence at the other end of the phone.

"Yes, maybe," came the reply.

"Adam, don't be frightened. We need to talk. I will get in my car this minute and drive to wherever you are. Where are you? Are you still in Cumbria?"

"No, I've gone away."

"Where are you?"

A pause.

"I'm in Douglas."

"Douglas? As in Douglas, in the Isle of Man?"

"Yes."

Mulholland absorbed this information. "I see. I will make sure I am in Douglas no later than three o'clock this afternoon. I will meet you at the local police station. Do you promise you will be there?"

"Yes, I promise."

"Otherwise we will have to undertake a police search to find you. Please leave your phone switched on."

"OK."

Mulholland replaced the receiver and called through to the office next door.

"Change of plan, Kate. I am going sight-seeing in the Isle of Man today. Get me on the first flight you can find."

4.

The little electric train juddered to a halt and there was a grinding sound as the brakes went on. Nick Potterton and Adam Meade had arrived at the summit station of the Snaefell mountain railway. They were at the highest point on the island.

Adam had been taciturn all the way from Douglas. They had travelled in Nick's car to the village of Laxey where Nick had parked close to the start of the railway. The car trip had been Nick's idea. He was interested to get to the top of Snaefell but the main motivation had been to ensure that Adam couldn't easily change his mind and walk away. Nick hadn't travelled half way across the Irish Sea to see his contact waltz off into the distance.

The train, a one carriage affair resembling a Victorian tramcar which still had its original nineteenth century wood panelling, took half an hour to climb the two thousand feet or so of height. The other travellers in the carriage took photos, oohed and aahed at the views and poured themselves coffee from flasks. Adam, beside the window, looked out at the countryside but said almost nothing.

"I've not been to the Isle of Man before," Nick proffered.

"Me neither," Adam replied.

"Any particular reason for choosing to come here?" Nick tried again.

Adam seemed to be in something of a reverie.

"It seemed like a good thing to do," he eventually replied.

"Yes. I think I understand. To get well away from things – and people."

The train paused briefly at a station half-way up the mountain.

"I didn't really think it through," Adam continued, turning away from the window to face Nick directly. "If you want the full story, the point is that Greensleeves has its legal address here. I'd got no way of knowing what my dad's death meant for the business, so I had this great idea. I thought I'd be able to go into the office and ask them what precisely was going on with the company."

Adam paused, and once again turned back to look out of the window.

"So what happened?" Nick prompted.

"I found the address all right, but it was just a nondescript office block. There were loads of company names on a plaque just inside the doorway. I asked someone who was in the building, and they more or less laughed at me. They said, 'oh no, this is just the accommodation address, nobody here knows anything about your business'."

Nick nodded. Adam went on.

"So after that I mooched around and wasted time. And then I saw on the news that I was a missing person. And I'm not quite sure why but I decided to text you. I didn't think you'd come."

"But I did," Nick replied.

"Yes."

The train was now pulling in to the final station, at the summit of Snaefell. Nick and Adam followed the other passengers outside. There was a cool wind on the mountain top but the day was beautiful, the sun glistening across the waters of the Irish Sea. Nick led the way from the station to the stone platform nearby which acted as a viewpoint.

"Nice views," he said, to break the silence.

"Yeah, nice enough."

"That's Snowdon," Nick said, pointing southwards. "The largest of those small bumps down there: that must be Snowdon."

Adam looked across at where Nick was pointing. "Yeah."

"And look, Adam, out there in the west. That must be Ireland over there." Far in the distance to the west, beyond the Isle of Man's own range of hills, were further distant peaks.

"I think those are the Mourne Mountains," Nick went on. "Slieve Donard's the highest. I ran up it in a fell race once," he added.

Adam seemed unimpressed. "Did you?" he asked without interest, following Nick's gaze.

"I've never been to Ireland," he went on eventually. "Maybe I'll get there some time."

"Maybe you will," Nick replied.

They both turned their gaze, looking northwards.

"We're lucky, the weather today is amazing for views," Nick said. He didn't really care what Adam thought, as far as he was concerned this was a moment to savour.

"What's over there?" Adam asked.

"Scotland. The Galloway hills. You can also see them on clear days from the Lake District." Nick paused.

"Of course when you're in the Lakes you can see Snaefell and the Isle of Man too," Nick went on. "The views work both ways. I've been on Pillar and on some of the other western Lakeland fells and looked across to where the whole island lies out in the sea, like some magical place half lost in the mist."

"So where's the Lake District from here?"

"There. To the east. Look. That must be Pillar. I wonder if that's Helvellyn behind? And of course that's Scafell Pike."

"Scafell Pike."

"Yes, the highest little pimple in England."

"The mountain my Dad was planning to climb."

"Yes."

There was a long pause. Nick eventually started the conversation again.

"You said you wanted to talk to me about your dad."

"I want the newspapers to explain what he was like," Adam replied.

He paused. "Do you know about my sister?"

"Your sister? I thought you had a younger brother."

"My sister was three years older than me. She died when I was nine. Leukaemia. My parents never really got over it, in fact they split up shortly afterwards. She ended up at the hospice near where we lived."

"The hospice your dad was fundraising for?"

"Yes. He'd have done anything for that place. Not that he mentioned the reason why he was so keen to fundraise, but I know he never forgot my sister."

"I see."

They were silent again, still looking across to the Cumbrian mountains in the distance.

"He was very unlucky to choose last weekend for the Three Peaks trip," Nick said. "I mean, because of the weather. The Lake District looks beautiful today, doesn't it," he added.

"I've arranged to talk to the police this afternoon, you know," Adam said, abruptly changing the subject.

"Have you?" Nick replied. He waited to see what Adam was going to say.

"Yes, in Douglas. The detective from Cumbria who's been looking into my dad's death is coming."

"George Mulholland?"

"Yes, that's his name. I spoke to him briefly this morning on the phone. He's flying out."

"He put out a missing person's alert for you, you know. I think he was worried that whoever had it in for your dad might have cornered you too. You need to tell him what you told me, when you rang me at the *Cumbrian Enquirer* that time. The fact that your dad felt at risk before he died. That you felt frightened yourself. It may help his enquiry."

Adam gave a mirthless laugh.

"Oh that story. Yes, I suppose they'll ask me about that."

"Sorry?"

"It seemed a good idea to say what I did to you at the time."

"And it doesn't seem a good idea any more?"

"Things have moved on."

Nick led Adam back to a seat close to the train station. They sat down.

"I wanted you to run something like that in your newspaper, so that the police would go looking for somebody who was out to do my dad in."

"Your dad had lots of debts, didn't he? So presumably there were creditors trying to get money from him."

"Yes, but that wasn't anything new."

Adam paused.

"I was trying to come up with an explanation for how my dad might have died. Something which didn't involve me in any way."

"You know what happened, Adam?"

This came out from Nick both as a question and as a statement.

Adam said nothing.

"It's good sometimes to get things off your chest," Nick continued. "And you did text me to say that you wanted to talk to me."

Adam had obviously come to a decision. "I worked in the kitchen until late last Saturday night," he started. "It was busy, we had loads of covers. I suppose the last diners left about ten fifteen and then we had to clean down. I don't know if you've ever worked in a kitchen but it's hard work.

"I finished the shift about eleven. Normally I'd have gone back to my room but last Saturday I didn't. My car was out the back of the hotel, it's an old Fiesta my mum helped me buy earlier in the year. I went out by the back door. It was absolutely pissing down."

"And you drove somewhere?"

"Yeah, I drove to Wasdale of course. Bloody hard to find, it was. Google said it would take an hour and a quarter from Keswick but it took me much longer. I got lost somewhere. I thought I might be late."

"To meet your dad?"

"Yes."

"You'd arranged it?"

"Yes, he'd told me he'd arrive there at 1am. Well, he didn't tell me directly. We'd agreed beforehand that he'd say what time he'd be getting there on Twitter. Of course I was reading his tweets."

"I see. So what happened?"

"I met him by his minibus but he told me to drive on a little way. He came and sat in the passenger seat. He'd managed to lock himself out of the bus with most of his stuff inside so he was in a pretty lousy mood anyway."

"You argued?"

"You could say that. He told me we had five minutes before he had to go. He told me I had to sign some documents."

"About Greensleeves?"

"Yes. And I said no."

"You didn't sign what he asked you to?"

"No. I'd always signed before. Like a dutiful son. But this time I said no." Adam paused momentarily. "I guess I've changed over

150

these last few months. Maybe I've grown up. My dad didn't realise. He still thought of me as his little boy. And he still thought that what he said went."

"I see."

"He was furious. He put his face..."

Adam stopped, and pulled himself together.

"He put his face right up against mine and said I was a fucking ungrateful son. Actually, it doesn't matter what he said. Just say that he was angry."

"But you still didn't sign"

"I still didn't sign. In fact, I think I argued back."

Adam paused yet again. "So what happened then was that my dad stormed off, slamming my car door behind him and rushing away. Into the rain. Most of his kit was still in the minibus but he had some sort of light jacket and a hand-torch."

"He'd have got soaked."

"Yes, but I guess he thought he'd catch up with the others. There was a big footpath just near where I'd parked and he hurried up that. I think he thought that was the way they'd gone. He'd forgotten that we'd driven further up the valley.

"So anyway when I realised that he was walking off into the night I ran after him and told him to come back. But he never said another word to me. He didn't look at me, he just kept marching on."

"And what did you do?"

"I tried keeping up with him for a while, but in the end I got soaked through myself and I went back to my car. I was still really angry with him. I thought, fuck you, what do I care if you get yourself lost on the hills."

Adam suddenly broke down and started sobbing. "I really did think that, you know. It's awful." He pulled himself together and carried on. "So I reversed the car and revved the engine and drove like a maniac all the way back to bloody Keswick. The police should have stopped me for dangerous driving. That's all you need to know."

"But what happened to your dad next?"

"I don't know. I suppose he left the path. I suppose he did get lost."

Nick didn't say anything.

"But then your newspaper came out. I was sure my dad hadn't been murdered, or at least not directly. There was nobody else around, it was dark as anything and wild weather. So I realised that if anyone was responsible for his death, it must be me. I shouldn't have let him leave my car like that.

"And when I saw your paper I tried to think of something that might stop the police finding out what had happened. It was all pretty stupid of me. I thought maybe I could get the police interested in a friend of my father's. He was called Geoff. It was a horrible thing to try to do."

"But now you've agreed to meet the police."

"Yes, I realised yesterday that I'd have to do that. In fact, the detective rang me himself. I know he's worried in case I don't show up, but I will," Adam continued. "I guess the truth always has to come out."

"Not always, no, but it looks like this time it will do."

"Yes," Adam paused.

"I think the train's about to leave," he went on. "I want to get off this mountain as quickly as I possibly can. Can you drive me back to Douglas?"

"Of course," Nick said. "And then? After all this is over? You'll need to take time to get over the past week. Are you going back to your job in Keswick?"

"They've sacked me," Adam shrugged. "That's fine. I've learned a lot already and I know I'm going to be good at my job. I might even see if there's anywhere here on the Isle of Man that will take me for the summer season. Get a job here."

"I hope you do." Nick took a final look at the distant Cumbrian fells and then followed Adam back to the railway carriage. They were just in time. The brakes were taken off and the little train made its way back down the hill.

It was another silent car journey, this time in the opposite direction to the way they had come in the morning.

"Drop me here," Adam said as they reached the clock tower in Douglas.

"OK." Nick slowed down and stopped. "Have you got all your things?"

"Yes." Adam reached across and shook his hand.

And then Adam shut Nick's car door, waved and disappeared into the Saturday crowd of shoppers.

5.

Booking the flight had been the easy bit. Kate Morgan had found George Mulholland a flight out of Manchester just after lunchtime which touched down at Ronaldsway airport on the Isle of Man early in the afternoon. It had meant a dash to Manchester airport to catch the plane, but he had done it.

Arranging with the local police to use an interview room had been somewhat less straightforward on a Saturday morning. Initially it seemed that nobody with the adequate seniority to make the decision was on duty. Eventually, though, that too had been taken care of. So George Mulholland found himself sitting in Douglas police station, idly checking the crime reports in a two-week old copy of the Isle of Man Examiner he had picked up at police reception and periodically looking at his watch.

At two minutes to three, the police station door opened and a young man with a small luggage bag came in. George Mulholland got to his feet.

"Hello," said the man. "I'm here."

"Hello, Adam," said George Mulholland in reply.

6.

Nick had found himself a hotel, a little to the north of Douglas's centre. From now on, he told himself, he wasn't a journalist on the trail of a story, he was a holidaymaker. He'd taken himself out for a gentle afternoon run and was in the hotel bar, having a first glass of red wine before making his way to the restaurant. He'd gone for one of the most expensive reds. Well why not, once in a while?

His mobile phone rang, and he checked the caller ID as he answered it.

"Hello, Lindsay," he said, a little surprised. "Good to hear from you."

"Er, yes," came Lindsay's reply. "Are you OK?"

"Absolutely fine. Having a very smooth glass of red wine in a hotel in the Isle of Man. Don't ask, it's too long a story. Where are you?"

"Actually Phil and I are outside your house, clutching a bottle of prosecco to celebrate your reinstatement in mountain rescue. I persuaded Pat earlier today. And… to have the meal with you that I think you mentioned. Both Phil and I have cycled over here so we're ready to eat a horse."

"Oh god, Lindsay. The meal I promised you both for Saturday evening."

"Yes, that's the one."

"I'm not at home."

"So it would appear. No nice stew waiting for us in the oven, then. No lasagne with crispy green salad. No freshly cooked lobster. Caviar's off, too."

"Will you ever forgive me?"

There was a long pause.

"Probably never," came the reply.

But outside Nick's darkened cottage Lindsay was smiling just a little.

"It's all right, I know a good takeaway in Ambleside," she added.

Also available from Gritstone Publishing

The Bad Step, by
Andrew Bibby

For Nick Potterton, the once high-flying London
journalist who has moved to the Cumbrian countryside,
Davie Peters' death should be just another story
to cover. But the longer he investigates, the more
disturbing questions he has to answer. Was the death
of one of England's most talented young athletes during
a traditional Lake District fell race as accidental as it
seemed? Or is somebody hiding the full story of what
happened at the rock-face high in the mountains that is
known as the Bad Step?